THE LEGACY SERIES

Evangelina, the protagonist of Dawn Burns' captivating collection *Evangelina Everyday*, has a life at least as rich as Walter Mitty—but, while Mitty dreams of blockbuster adventures, Evangelina dreams of what feels to her like the boldest fantasy of all: getting to somehow be her full self. Burns renders this vivid inner world with compassion and a sharp eye for emotional detail. As a result, *Evangelina Everyday* is an invitation to hope—to hope that what is bound can become free.

—DAVID EBENBACH
author of *Miss Portland* and *How to Mars*

Dawn Burns is a master of symbol and metaphor. Through her carefully connected collection of vignettes and stories, Evangelina emerges as no everyday protagonist. She is so unique, memorable, and relatable that I find myself in still moments noticing some tiny detail before me as suddenly significant and I wonder, "What would Evangelina make of this?" The name means "good news." *Evangelina Everyday* is good news indeed for readers who savor a character-driven, exquisitely written story.

—JAN MAHER
author of *Earth As It Is* and *Heaven, Indiana*

Dawn Burns writes interiority with a talent that can fill a moment— any moment—with unbound wonder. Her voice is subtly profound, building word upon clause until each sentence becomes a tiny, teeming world. Evangelina's realms contain quiet roars and deceptive calms. They are as pure and polished as the insides of shells, but likewise kept within hardened façades and protected by spikes. These stories invite you to lean in and listen for Evangelina to sound herself out, because the moments of her life are always something to hear, or flow through, or dive deep within—say, the day on the lake when Evangelina tells her cousin, "I wish you wouldn't pull me under like that. I could drown, you know," and her cousin responds, "Then you'd better take a deep breath before I do." Take a deep breath and read this book. It will float that breath right away.

—CURTIS VanDONKELAAR
author of *Bad Man Love Stories*

With soaring visions of the undetected visions of an ordinary woman and a merciless eye for the surreal side of reality, Dawn Burns spins a tale that leaps from lyricism to bitter and back again. Mix poetic narrative with Burns' ability to explore everyday provocations exploding into unacceptable truths, and you'll have *Evangelina Everyday*.

—RANDY SUSAN MEYERS
bestselling author of *Waisted*

These epiphanic, tightly focused, sublimely rendered meditations are secular prayer proems that trace the elegantly ecstatic patterns captured on the flat glass of cloud chambers. These brief pieces are, everyone, another origin story in Evangelina's evolution. Every day is a different Homeric Hymn, and each day is greeted by a unique shade of rosy-fingered Dawn floating on the illuminated manuscript of the wine-dark sentences of seeing. *Evangelina Everyday* has the unerring accuracy of an atomic clock and an eye more open than the new Webb Space Telescope out there capturing the decayed infrared light of the billion-year-old Big Bang.

—MICHAEL MARTONE
author of *Plain Air: Sketches of Winesburg, Indiana*

Evangelina Everyday

A Novel in Stories

Dawn Burns

CORNERSTONE PRESS
UNIVERSITY OF WISCONSIN-STEVENS POINT

Cornerstone Press, Stevens Point, Wisconsin 54481
Copyright © 2022 Dawn Burns
www.uwsp.edu/cornerstone

Printed in the United States of America.

Library of Congress Control Number: 2021951773
ISBN: 978-1-7377390-4-3

This is a work of fiction. Names, characters, businesses, places, events, and incidents are either the products of the author's imagination or used in a fictitious manner. Any resemblance to actual persons, living or dead, or actual events is purely coincidental.

"Evangelina Contemplates 'PRIME SPACE'" first appeared in *Women Under Scrutiny: An Anthology of Truths, Essays, Poems, Stories & Art*. Edited by Nancy MacDonald. Brooklyn Girl Books. 2019. Commentary and compilation by Randy Susan Meyers.

Cornerstone Press titles are produced in courses and internships offered by the Department of English at the University of Wisconsin–Stevens Point.

DIRECTOR & PUBLISHER   EXECUTIVE EDITOR   SENIOR EDITORS
Dr. Ross K. Tangedal   Jeff Snowbarger   Lexie Neeley & Monica Swinick

SENIOR PRESS ASSISTANTS
Emma Fisher & Gavrielle McClung

PRESS STAFF
Rosie Acker, Rhiley Block, Kala Buttke, Grace Dahl, Patrick Fogarty, Kyra Goedken, Brett Hill, Amanda Leibham, Annika Rice, Abbi Rohde, Bethany Webb

For Mary Catherine

CONTENTS

Evangelina Feels Adrift

"I feel adrift," Evangelina said, sitting at the kitchen table reading but not really reading the *Elkhart Truth* as Russell went about his business preparing a fire for the night because on cold December nights, that is just what they had come to do over their twenty-one years of marriage.

"Go put a sweater on," Russell said, not looking up from the assortment of shredded newspaper, dryer lint, and twigs he meticulously saved for nights like this.

Evangelina folded over the *Truth* and pushed herself back from the table, stood, and walked the short hall to the long hallway closet full of neglected jackets, coats, and sweaters, only one of which, her worn burgundy sweater, appealed to her. Evangelina felt both heavy and not standing there. She slipped the sweater from the hanger and shrugged herself into it. She felt, she thought, both heavy and not.

It did not matter that Russell had misheard her, that he had thought she had said "a draft." Evangelina did not need to correct Russell because she knew she couldn't, really, ever correct him, that she could never explain herself to his satisfaction and she was so very tired from trying.

As she pulled the sweater snug around her body she said softly and only to herself, "I feel a drift."

Evangelina Prays for *Downton Abbey*

In the dark of her bedroom, Evangelina McQuarry lay awake, her husband Russell snoring fitfully beside her like, she thought, a congested elephant. Evangelina opened her eyes. Evangelina closed her eyes. Evangelina concluded that whether her eyes were opened or closed made no difference whatsoever. In her face she felt a tightness, a sort of grimace that began at her lips' outer edges and coursed upwards around her eyes and to her forehead, making furrows she could feel if not see. Briefly, Evangelina wondered about her sudden onset of wrinkles, ones she could see when she looked in the bathroom mirror in the mornings. Ones she chose not to see by not looking.

Evangelina told herself to stop thinking, willed herself to focus first on her inhalation of breath, then her exhalation—this being the only practice she had retained from her yoga class six years ago. *Breathe in. Breathe out.* She felt the tightness in her face disappear, felt her skin loosen just a little. She pulled her arms out from under the blankets and stretched them full length on top of the comforter and at her sides. The way she liked to sleep. The only way she could. *Breathe in. Breathe out. Breathe in. Breathe out. This is good,* she thought, then reprimanded herself for thinking and relaxed her hold on the blanket. Evangelina tried again. *Breathe in. Breathe out. Breathe in.* Then Russell rolled over and jerked the blanket out from under her arms, leaving her body exposed, her breathing meditation broken.

She shouldn't have been irritated. Evangelina knew it wasn't Russell's fault, but still, after twenty-one years of sharing a bed with this man, she was tired of having to fight for covers, for her own comfort. Evangelina felt again the tightness in her face, and when Russell combined a sleep-snort with a fart, she grabbed hold of the comforter and yanked hard. She hated everything about this moment but she wasn't going to say a word because she never did. Soon enough it would be morning.

Evangelina rolled over on her side. 1:26 in green digital light blazed out and she thought this was the worst possible time to be awake, but quite possibly the very best time to pray because, really, what else was there for her to do but return to this relic of her religious upbringing in the middle of her sleepless nights? And though it did not matter in the dark whether Evangelina opened or closed her eyes, she closed them tightly and waited for the names and faces of those most present in her life to click across the screen of her mind as they always did, as though they were slides in an old slide carousel of the sort nobody, not even Evangelina, used anymore.

Mother. Of course, mother. *What sort of daughter doesn't pray for her mother?* Mother had asked for prayer for her gout that very morning on the telephone during their exceedingly long conversation about the rainy weather and weekly Kroger sales and whether Evie (for Evie and not Evangelina was the name her mother had given her at birth) had yet managed to get tickets for that program at the hospital. "You remember, Evieee," her mother said, drawing out the last "e" like she was a bleating goat and not Evangelina's mother after all, "the one about that tick disease—what is it they call it? Blimey disease?" Her mother had been sure to inform Evangelina that her gout was acting up in reaction to their Sunday lunch at Red Lobster, Evangelina and Russell's choice. Her mother had wanted instead to go to Ponderosa, but as Evangelina and Russell were driving, the final choice came down to them. Evangelina did not for herself regret the cheddar biscuits or the Admiral's Feast but thinking just then in the dark about it all, she did feel a twinge of guilt given the seafood's impact on her mother. *Dear God, please make Mother's gout go away. Heal it for good so we can all just be done with it, or at least make it better for now so she can get out of the house tomorrow, go for a walk. And the tickets. God, help me remember those tickets in the morning.* Still, Evangelina knew she would forget. Again.

Duchess jumped on the bed and curled against her side. Evangelina reflected that at seven years of age, her orange tabby was the same age in cat years as she was in human years, and she knew this because just two days before she had out of curiosity completed the calculations online only to discover that Duchess at seven was equal to her at 44. Evangelina didn't exactly pray for Duchess but she did pet her, scratching first behind her ears and then up and down her spine, holding on to the impossible hope that Duchess would live long past her own middle age. Evangelina did not like the idea of being lonely and alone in the world.

Breathe in. Breathe out.

The next face to appear was, well, it wasn't even a face, really, not even a name, just the voice of the NPR reporter who had told about the medical student in India who had been raped on the bus and then died in the days following the first report. What was her name? Evangelina wished she knew the girl's name as names seemed to matter somehow, but Evangelina didn't know the girl's name or have an image of her face, only knew that the story—just the idea, the brutality of it—had sickened her for days. That such a horror should happen in the world mattered to her and also to God. *God!* And that was all she could think to pray.

Evangelina opened her eyes and found they had adjusted enough to the dark of the room so that she could make out the looming shapes of the closet doors and bureau drawers that stuck out at odd angles. She could get out of bed and close them, Evangelina knew, but instead she closed her eyes again, cleared her mind, waited to remember something or somebody she had forgotten in prayer, and that was when Lady Edith Crawley, who was her favorite of Lord Crawley's daughters at Downton Abbey, drifted into view.

Soon after, the others followed. Matthew and Lady Mary, boring as they were, and poor Lady Sybil who had married Tom Branson for love and did she now regret it, playing second fiddle to the whole of Ireland as she was? Lord Grantham, certainly, his needs went so unregarded, she thought, and she remembered when he had had his almost-affair with that maid (whatever was her name?) with the young son who had been widowed by the war. Evangelina wondered now that all that mess was over whether Lord Grantham thought of her still, whether he was glad he had felt something like desire if only for a moment.

Prayers for Mrs. Hughes and Mrs. Patmore were easy, and she thanked God that Mrs. Hughes did not have cancer, prayed that neither Mrs. Hughes nor she would know the pain of that. And wasn't it remarkable that Mrs. Patmore had gotten her eyes fixed so she could see to cook! Would have been sad for Downton and also for her, she knew, if Mrs. Patmore had been lost to Downton Abbey.

It did not seem in Evangelina's mind the least bit odd to lift up Ethel who had taken up prostitution since leaving Downton. Certainly, Evangelina wasn't fond of her, never liked Ethel from the beginning, in fact, and in some ways she was satisfied to see Ethel in such disgrace after all her high-talk about movie stars and such. Sort of satisfying, but not fully. Surely Ethel was deserving of some good in her life. She had never harmed anybody but herself really, not like Thomas. *Oh, Thomas.* Evangelina kicked at the wadded-up sheet under the comforter, kicked it out of the way. She could hardly even think of Thomas let alone pray for him. The best she could do was surrender him into God's hands and repress her own desire that God should wring his neck, recognizing even as she prayed that without Thomas a huge part of the tension of the show would be gone, and then what motivation would she have to watch? *Everything that happens has a purpose,* she prayed as if praying this could make it true, then chastised herself for praying for characters in what she knew was a television show, none of them the least bit real though often she wished they could be more real than this snoring, farting husband beside her.

Russell turned toward his edge of the bed and Evangelina felt the comforter go with him. Evangelina could do without any of the other blankets—the worn flannel sheet, the coarse wool blanket—but she could not do without the down comforter, so she grabbed hold with both hands, giving it a quick yank as she rolled further toward her edge of the bed taking not all of the comforter, but almost her fair share.

That was when Evangelina thought again of Lady Edith, Lady Edith alone in her grand Downton Abbey bed. Lady

Edith, alone. To be sure, Evangelina knew, in the grand scheme of things Lord Anthony with his useless hand had been no great loss, just as he had been no great prize to begin with. Of course, Evangelina would have been reluctant to tell Edith this, having seen her grief-stricken at being jilted at the altar, and she could understand that. Still, Edith had to herself the entire bed with no one to steal her down comforter, and certainly down comforters would have been what all the beds at Downton had. She caught her own pun—*Downton, down*. How clever of her. Unintended, of course, but still very much clever, which was the best sort of cleverness, the way it just came rolling out of her mind so naturally. Cleverness was, Evangelina knew, one of her better qualities, even if Russell could not appreciate it. In truth, that Russell couldn't appreciate her cleverness made her feel all the more clever.

Evangelina pulled the comforter up to her chin, feeling the seam at the end and the silky tag remnant that had read "made in Laos" before she had snipped it. Evangelina recalled the day she had rescued the comforter from the Kohl's clearance shelf, marked as it was with the big yellow CLEARANCE star, which looked cheap in the way clearance items were meant to look to set themselves apart from the other merchandise and produce a hint of shame outweighed only by a customer's excitement. But this comforter, well, it really was nice, and 80% off made it perfectly within her price range, which was over $20 yet under $50. Orange was not her favorite color, she did not think, but then she saw no reason to be picky as color did not matter so very much when one was asleep in the dark.

Evangelina thought again of Lady Edith lying in the dark under her downy Downton Abbey comforter and of how Edith had wanted so desperately to be married, and to Lord Anthony of all people. And now here Edith was at the end of season three, episode two, and she wouldn't be married after all. All Edith's mother had thought to say was, "You are being tested. Being tested only makes you stronger." Evangelina hadn't liked those words any more than she had liked Russell saying, "Oh, for Christ's sake! Why can't you just get over it!" when her friend Rose from yoga had moved to Canada and Evangelina had been so sad she'd stopped cooking and ordered Chinese takeout every night for two weeks.

God, take away Lady Edith's grief! Evangelina prayed, for Evangelina, who still sometimes cried about Rose, knew grief when she saw it.

Still, Evangelina couldn't blame Lord Anthony for bailing on the whole marriage business. Hadn't Edith used the word "project" to describe him? "You'll be my lifelong project," she had said, or something very much like that. Well, now that marrying Lord Anthony wasn't even an option, maybe now Edith could get around to being a voice for women's rights, for the vote. And maybe one day Edith could find somebody to really love for love's sake and not because she felt so godforsaken awkward and purposeless like an ugly duckling who had yet to discover her swan heritage. Though Evangelina worried it was heretical to wish such a thing, still she wished for Edith to be the one sister who didn't marry and was happy about it. This was a wish, though, and not a prayer as she did not at all see how God entered into such matters.

A thought Evangelina did not want sparked and threatened to flare, but she tamped it down. In his sleep, Russell farted the long, slow, squeaky sort of fart that creeps out through any gap in bedclothes it can find, seeking to offend. Without raising the comforter, Evangelina gripped the fabric with her hands and clutched it even tighter around her, tucking it under her body until she was snug as a caterpillar. Then a spark flared and Evangelina felt a sudden and sharp resentment toward Russell, not exactly for anything he had done to her let alone for the fart, but for what had happened earlier that night when he plopped down beside her on the couch while she was watching *Downton Abbey* because she had not joined him in the bedroom for sex.

The truth of the matter was, Evangelina would have liked to be able to enjoy *Downton Abbey* with Russell. She indulged in pleasant daydreams about she and Russell sitting side by side, she leaning into him as they experienced a shared connection over *Downton*, a show that might have brought them back into sync, given them common ground. But what had Russell done? Just as Lady Sybil was standing inside a phone booth on a darkened street in Ireland saying something about having gotten out without being followed, Russell reached his clammy hand down her striped pajama top and groped her. Evangelina had pulled his hand out away from her breasts and placed it firmly on his leg. There might be times for such things, but certainly her husband of all people should have known that 9:15 on a Sunday evening was not the time, so she had said, "Russell! Not now! I am *watching*!" Russell had settled back into the couch (chastened, she hoped) hands in his lap, and began to grumble, at first to himself, but then aloud.

"Where's the sex, Evie?" Russell asked when Tom arrived at Downton and he and Sybil embraced. Evangelina hated how her husband called her Evie, hated that he did not take seriously her desire to be called Evangelina. Was that really such a hard change to make? She had made this change herself two seasons ago, three episodes into the first season, not because she was obsessed with the show but because the name Evangelina just, well, it just fit her better. She could understand her mother calling her Evie and let that go. After all, her mother had given her that name and Evangelina was a good daughter, devoted to remembering her mother in prayer in the middle of sleepless nights and to honoring her in all the ways good daughters should. But Russell? Why could her husband not respect her desire to be called Evangelina? Had he asked to be called Rutherford, Evangelina surely would have honored his request.

"My God!" Russell had shouted, "Don't these people ever fuck?"

"Shh!" Evangelina had reprimanded, regretting now that her husband had sat down beside her in the first place. If Russell couldn't behave, he did not deserve to sit beside her and watch *Downton Abbey*.

"If not sex, can't they at least have dragons, even just one dragon?" Without knowing exactly why, a swell of hurt filled Evangelina but she did not say as much to Russell—he would not understand. Surely, she had suffered *Game of Thrones* for Russell's sake. Was he really incapable of caring like her about the upstairs and downstairs lives of Downton Abbey's residents in their everyday complexities? *God give me strength!*

Breathe in. Breathe out.

Evangelina knew now she wouldn't sleep. Couldn't sleep. Still, she tried to get into a rhythm that might allow it, tried to let her thoughts enter, pass through, and leave with the nonjudgmental awareness she'd once possessed when practicing yoga, but all that was behind and also beyond her now, and wasn't that really for the best?

Evangelina rolled over, looked at the curve of Russell's back underneath the comforter, felt a mixture of tenderness and hostility as though she would have loved just then to fit her body around his were it not for a prickling agitation that felt the way the Dowager Countess looked, that felt uncomfortably proper even when she knew there was some spark of loveliness left in her. Evangelina rolled onto her back and stared up into the darkness.

Nonsense. She thought. *I'm just full of nonsense.* Evangelina knew *Downton Abbey* was just a television show. She knew that none of the characters even existed, least of all Edith, so how could praying for them make any difference whatsoever, and why had she even started down this road on tonight of all nights? Still, she felt certain that her prayers were not in vain, that these people who lived at Downton, whether upstairs or downstairs or cast out to prostitution or prison really did have souls like her very own, that they were real souls even if they were not real people.

She turned her head to look again at Russell, remembered him calling her a Walter Mitty when it came to Downton Abbey. Evangelina had known generally what he had meant, but still had googled "Walter Mitty" to make sure she remembered that story properly before ruling out that she was no such character. Not only would she never say "puppy biscuit" out of context in a public place, she also was not lost in a daydream believing herself to be a fourth Grantham daughter. She did not pretend to live at Downton, nor did she wish to. And as much as Evangelina loved the downstairs occupants of Downton, she knew she would have no room for them in her three-bedroom ranch-style home built on a slab in Elkhart, Indiana. There was no downstairs. There was no upstairs. There was only . . . only what? Only this. There was only this and that was fine, Evangelina told herself. Why, Evangelina didn't even favor furniture or fixtures from the post-Edwardian period. She was happy enough with whatever she could find on clearance at Kohl's regardless of whether it all matched or even came in her favorite colors, which were . . . what were they? Green and blue? Yellow? She couldn't remember having once cared about colors, couldn't remember having once had a favorite, and why should she because the only colors of Kohl's clearance items were nobody's favorites.

I just like the show, Evangelina thought to herself. *Does that make me a fanatic? No.* She knew that it did not, and she knew it because a fanatic would have owned the first two seasons on Blu-ray and had plans to own the third, but Evangelina owned none, had only watched them faithfully on PBS channel 34. What's more, she had not purchased nor even received any of the numerous collector's books as gifts, though Russell would have been thoughtful to have given them. She had only briefly looked at the Amazon preview of *The Unofficial Downton Abbey Cookbook: From Lady Mary's Crab Canapes to Mrs. Patmore's Christmas Pudding—More than 150 Recipes from Upstairs and Downstairs* because she stumbled upon it searching for a recipe for chocolate crumpets. Evangelina had not even downloaded the *Downton Abbey* iPad app for ninety-nine cents, and this would have been easy enough had she wanted, had she even had an iPad. The most she had done was asked to be called Evangelina, which was certainly within her rights, was it not?

Walter Mitty, my foot, Evangelina thought, and extended her leg so that her toenails scraped the back of Russell's right calf. At this Russell shifted, mumbled into the darkness. Evangelina pulled her leg back into position, patted Duchess, asked herself, *Am I a Walter Mitty? Do I wish I could live at Downton?* She pondered. *No. I just want the best for them.* This is what she had said when Russell first made the comparison, and then she had added, "I learn about history when I watch *Downton Abbey.* There's just so much I didn't know before about these people, this time period, that now I know."

But Evangelina knew this was a lie. The Crawleys could have been living on a starship in the 25th century and she would still have found them interesting. She had no reason to care about them. She simply did because of who they were.

Breathe in. Breathe out.

Evangelina thought again about her mother and the tickets. She wanted to buy them for her tomorrow, take her mother to the hospital program. Well, maybe "wanted" was too strong a word, but she felt she should and knew in the end she would because she was a good daughter. Evangelina had all the reason in the world to care about her mother, after all, and even about Russell. What kind of daughter would she be if she didn't?

What kind of daughter? What kind of wife?

"I'm a useful spinster!" In her darkness, Evangelina remembered Lady Edith crying out these words to her maidservant Anna the morning after her abandonment, and that word . . . not spinster but that other one . . . "useful," did not so much stir something in Evangelina as grieve her. "I'm a *useful* spinster. Good at helping out. That is my role. And spinsters get up for breakfast."

Breakfast. Evangelina did not want to think ahead to daylight when she would get up for a bowl of cold raisin bran and a cup of hot coffee tempered with a splash of evaporated milk, did not even want to think at all about getting up with not so much as a maidservant to talk to. Sure, Russell would be there, but he was not so much company as . . . Evangelina didn't know as what exactly but maybe as furniture. At least Lady Edith felt useful, thought Evangelina. At least Lady Edith had a role she knew how to live. Were it not for Duchess needing to be fed, Evangelina thought she might have nothing useful to do at all.

Russell rolled over and Evangelina studied his face. His eyelids flickered and closed. His upper lip curled and she recognized his quick smile from what seemed a lifetime ago, a look she only now saw while he slept, his smile having been replaced by a smirk long ago. Evangelina closed her eyes again, felt his exhale of breath against her face. *Breathe in.* Her breath got all tight inside her chest and she wanted to hold it inside forever as if she could hold together all of her scattered, uncertain self.

If she cried Russell might wake, and then what? She wouldn't be good for anything then, but then she wasn't good for anything now and wasn't that just the point? Lady Edith might have been a spinster, but she was useful, and Evangelina was . . . well, she didn't know what she was and she didn't know how to live. Was that it? Had she once known and forgotten? Had she never figured it out? She didn't even know that anymore. Mostly, though, she was just tired.

Her favorite color . . . what was it?

Evangelina Goes to a Christmas Cookie Exchange

The morning after the Christmas cookie exchange, staring into the unlidded box of cookies on the kitchen table before her, Evangelina asked herself, "Was last night fun?"

Evangelina could not decide.

Waiting for her morning coffee to brew, Evangelina stared at the cookies in what she recognized to be a poor attempt to draw her attention away from the befuddling nightmare that had been the party and onto the object of the party itself made so reliably of flour, sugar, butter, chocolate, mint, molasses, smears of peanut butter, and pinches of salt, teaspoons of baking soda and baking powder, pounds of powdered sugar and ounces of cream cheese, and probably—somewhere in some batter somewhere—rum and Kahlua and who knew what else.

On the whole, Evangelina did not know what to call these cookies, and this bothered her more than she could admit. Evangelina's contemplation of ingredients made her stomach lurch, so she pulled back, broadened her perspective, focused on the cookies as complete and separate entities, searching for the ones she had names for—monster cookies, raspberry thumbprint cookies (for which she knew the name because it had been displayed), peanut butter fudge (not technically a cookie, but still she was pleased to find it on the table), and most reliably, peanut butter blossoms—those sugar-sanded peanut butter wonders affixed with Hershey kisses in their dimpled tops.

Four people out of the twenty-three at the party had brought peanut butter blossoms, so proportionally, Evangelina had ended up with more peanut butter blossoms than any other cookie. Three of the four, she remembered from last night's circuit around the Christmas tree wrapping-papered pool table, had used the full-sized individually-wrapped kisses, and one had used the miniature kisses found in bags in the Martin's baking aisle just above the coconut and below the Nestle chips. Evangelina, though she had not said this at the party full of strangers, felt that using prepackaged miniature kisses without the silver foil wrappers was a sort of cheating, a kind of laziness. Had her friends Krista and Tobi Ann showed up to the party, Evangelina would have whispered this clever insight to them, but they had not showed, had they? Evangelina winced, tamped down a spark of betrayal. Martyrdom did not suit her, after all.

Evangelina scanned the box in search of the lemon-frosted sugar cookie and the silver-dollar sized chocolate cookie with peppermint frosting, both of which had, when the cookies were finally exchanged, looked appealing even in the yellow glow of the Purdue University lights of the hostess's basement. Evangelina could find neither, and she was reluctant to dig and add to the sad erosion of cookies that had already begun.

Evangelina shuddered. Had she really been at that dreadful woman's house for four and a half hours? Had she really been all alone amidst strangers who spent the night downing Jell-O shots topped with vodka-infused whipped cream and talking about . . . what . . . what had they talked about? Turning over some variety of a no-bake cookie in search of peanut butter fudge, Evangelina tried to remember, but all she could recall was an hour-long three-way cost-comparison of athletic uniforms—football, volleyball, and basketball—for the guests' high performing high school varsity children. Evangelina, who had no children and found Russell quite enough work to care for, had nothing to add. How was it she had even been invited to this party, she asked herself again.

Oh, yes. Krista and Tobi Ann had said she would get cookies enough to freeze and pull out two weeks from now for Christmas without having to bake any more. And had Evangelina's two friends, friends she had thought before last night to be good friends, really not shown up at all?

"We hate this party," Krista had said when they ganged up to invite her.

"But the cookies are good," Tobi Ann countered, "And I'm bringing molasses crinkles, which I know you love."

"Come on! We'll keep each other company," pleaded Krista. "We'll leave before they start doing shots and getting stupid."

"We'll leave before she gives her house tour," Tobi Ann said.

"Oh, God! The tour! We'll leave before she can even suggest a group selfie in her walk-in shower," Krista promised.

What was it that Krista and Tobi Ann had promised repeatedly?

"If you go, we'll go, but we're not walking in there alone. Eat some snacks, have a glass of wine, get the cookies, and run."

And what was it that had happened, Evangelina thought with hardly a crumb of bitterness, hardly even caring that on Facebook she had been tagged in a photo standing awkwardly with a group of drunk women in a walk-in marble shower at the home of a woman who was not and never would be her friend.

What was it again that had happened, Evangelina asked herself as though the evidence in the box in front of her was not enough to convince her even now.

Evangelina had gone to the Christmas cookie exchange, but her so-called friends never showed.

Evangelina Contemplates "Prime Space"

PRIME SPACE.

That's what the hanging sign said, white and rectangular with simple yet bold red letters, standing out against old brick and moving with the force of January winds and then back in place.

PRIME SPACE.

What did that even mean?

From her window seat at the high counter in Yeast of Eden, her hometown coffee shop that Evangelina knew well but did not love, was incapable somehow of loving, Evangelina watched the sign for a sign. Tuesday mornings were like that for her. She hugged her white coffee mug with her hands, raised it to her lips, sipped, set it down again. She liked the feel of the warm mug against her palms more than she liked the taste of bitter coffee in her mouth.

At the counter two seats to her right sat a young man, a college student by the looks of him with his blue Laplander hat pulled down tight over his ears and his human anatomy text spread out in front of him, opened to a spread-legged drawing of female genitalia, all pink and flat and frightening. Evangelina had always hated those kinds of pictures, how vivid yet flat they were with names of body parts in bold black ink and thin lines extending out to almost but not quite touch, leaving on the page a gap of white between the words and the pictures. *Clitoris. Vulva. Labia. Vagina.* Evangelina couldn't help but notice, and in noticing a memory crept up of finding *Bailliere's Atlas of Female Anatomy* in her father's study when she was just a child no older than ten. *Bailliere's*, a thin blue volume, had on its cover an armless marble statue with soulless eyes. Her fingers remembered the heaviness she felt turning over page after page, and on each page finding numbers that corresponded with words for all the parts of her, pictures and words for what was, she knew, her own body, herself. *Uterus. Fallopian Tubes. Egg.* Those words and pictures like impossible alien worlds that existed beneath her own skin, that went deeper even than the ropes of muscles all braided together sketched in fine pencil and colored pink on other pages.

Evangelina remembered feeling that she should not know those words, but those words once known could not be unknown. Evangelina remembered feeling that her mother would not, had she known, have allowed her to sit spread-legged on the floor of her bedroom, looking in the mirror at those corresponding parts of herself and saying their names in a whisper, like she was studying for a test she would surely never have to take. But Evangelina did look, and she did touch, and she then knew what to call all the parts of herself, even the parts deep inside that she couldn't see, even though they were words to a language she shouldn't know. And what's more, because they were pictures in her father's book, Evangelina knew they were words her father had known about parts of her before she had even known them for herself and that had made her feel … what? What had it made her feel? Evangelina couldn't say exactly, because that was not how her feelings worked, not, she thought, how her feelings were supposed to work. Feelings couldn't ever really be labelled or defined, not like the pictures in her father's book. All she knew, all she had known, was that the book was a thing to be put back on its shelf exactly as it had been situated—spine even with the books beside it—before she had even entered her father's study, and so she did. Not that that could undo her knowing, scrub her mind of those pictures and words the way her mother on her hands and knees scrubbed the green linoleum kitchen floor, wanting it to look as new as it had the day it was laid down. No. Not like that.

Evangelina was staring. She hadn't meant to stare, but the student in the Laplander hat who sat with his right hand on his chin and his left hand raised with a yellow highlighter glanced back at her now, smiled, so she moved her eyes to a thread on her burgundy sweater that she had been meaning to cut but hadn't. She gave the thread a quick tug but it didn't break, only began an unraveling. What did it matter? Christmas was already over, so why should she care? Still, her feeling was that it did. She smoothed the thread back down and looked up and out of the window to PRIME SPACE, the sign never still for long, subject to each gust of wind, large or small.

Evangelina knew she looked suspicious, guessed that the student could read her mind, but she couldn't look at him to know for sure, so instead she raised her mug to her lips and took a sip so casually she knew she couldn't possibly look casual. The wind only seemed to blow one direction today, as maybe it always did without her ever really thinking about it, but that sign, PRIME SPACE was constantly being pushed away in the direction of the cars travelling along the street in the direction that took them out of town. A westerly direction? An easterly one? She didn't know. Maybe it was north, even. Or south. Evangelina never could tell about those larger directions in the world, the ones a compass could have told her about had she had one, had she cared. And she did, really, sort of care right now, which she found odd because usually she didn't. She usually wasn't bothered about not knowing her place in the world and which direction she was headed, but just now for whatever reason she wanted to know in which direction the wind was blowing, which direction it was pushing the PRIME SPACE sign. Russell would have cared about such things, she knew. Her husband always cared about such things. And he would have already figured out the direction because those were things he knew without even needing a compass.

She lifted again the white mug to her lips, the coffee now cooler than the surrounding air, and while this was something she minded, she felt no desire to go to the trouble of standing and walking around the man with the Laplander hat and the anatomy book and over to the counter against the yellow wall where six varieties of coffee waited, any one of which could have warmed her up, but only one of which, the decaf house blend, she could have chosen for herself.

Evangelina had looked outside and she had looked at the student, but for the first time that day Evangelina lifted her eyes and noticed an overlarge peppermint candy hanging from the coffee shop ceiling. This fake yet decorative candy the size of a medium pizza was wrapped in clear plastic and hanging from a red ribbon that reached up to a row of glowing blue pinecones in fake pine garland. The decorations, though thematically awkward, Evangelina thought, were pretty. In fact, they were the sort of decorations she might look for at Kohl's for 50% off the day after Christmas, the sort she might even be lucky enough to find, though not enough of them to stretch out across her front room window, not with all the shoppers she would be elbowing. Still, these lights would be something to look for. There was also sparkly red beaded garland, like Mardi Gras beads but more dignified, looped at uneven intervals—some three inches, some five, and so on—throughout the fake greenery. That added a nice splash of color and looked good with the peppermints and occasional red bulbs. Yes, that would be nice. But maybe Michaels would be a better place to shop, she thought, even than Kohl's. Michaels always had so much of that stuff after Christmas.

Evangelina's neck began to hurt. That was the way bodies worked at her age when one part would do something for just a little too long. She grew aware of a slight stretching in the skin of her neck, and a small cramp in her lower back. Slowly, and with pain, she tucked her chin to her chest, then rolled her head all the way to the right where her eyes met the two-foot tree at the spot where the front window met at an angle with the wall then all, no, not all, half-way to the right where the student was sitting, not studying now, his cheek smackdab against the oversized vagina, asleep. Had he no shame? No shame whatsoever? The sight made Evangelina terribly uncomfortable, even if her primary view was the back of his Laplander hat, which was bright blue and had a door on it and looked like an old phone booth, or something very much like it. She knew from the moment she saw the hat that it was a cultural reference to a television show that was not a part of her culture, but that was all she knew, and she hated feeling left out of a secret.

Evangelina wanted to go and shake him awake, or at least slide the book out from under his face and close it. Books could become pillows to tired students, even she knew that, but the least he could have done was close it first.

Evangelina Caresses Dough

Once in a very great while, Evangelina touched something that gave her pleasure. This morning, it was the soft, round balls of pie crust dough, lightly floured, smoother than velvet, ready to be rolled and rested in Pyrex pans.

Evangelina Takes Her Husband for a Medical Procedure

Evangelina did not like the way the chair in Dr. Flandel's surgical suite hit her just below her shoulder blades, and she did not like having to watch Russell, laid out in his blue-striped hospital gown, fondling the doctor's stress ball, a transparent bag of silicone imprinted with the words, "SAMPLE. DO NOT IMPLANT!"

"Come over here and get a feel of this, Evangelina," Russell said, squeezing and unsqueezing the breast implant the doctor had left with him. "Now this … THIS is a boob!"

Evangelina willed herself to stay seated and to keep her mouth shut, distracting herself from her rising rage by pressing her back against the chair and rolling her shoulder blades over the top, then down and back into place. This she did over and over, directing herself to look anywhere but at Russell who was still fondling the breast in a bag, but wherever she looked in the small room she could still see him out of the corner of her eye.

Evangelina looked at the clock on the wall. 10:14. Dr. Flandel was now fourteen minutes late from when Russell's procedure was supposed to have started. A nurse had come in on time to check Russell's vitals and then the doctor had stopped by briefly to hand Russell the implant while he waited. "Feels real," Russell had said, jiggling the disembodied breast in his cupped hands, and the doctor had said, "I know, right?" and then Russell had said, "And it can't even say no," to which they both laughed.

Evangelina hated them both, felt they deserved each other. She couldn't wait for Russell's proctologist to return so she could leave and he could suffer.

Evangelina Watches the Sky

From her bedroom window, Evangelina, through branches still bare in late March, watched the pink of early morning sky fade to white and gave herself brief permission to long for green for the branches, to mourn the loss of pink for the sky, to feel deeply the colorless length of the day ahead, and still to hope for a blazing orange sunset at day's end.

Evangelina Remembers Yoga

Walking through the park, Evangelina saw a cherry tree in full pink blossom and beneath the tree a woman moving her body in a way she recognized, a way she herself had once moved, a way for which she had a name.

Surya Namaskar. Sun Salutation.

The woman moved her hands from heart's center to above and then behind her head, arching her back and pushing her hips forward. Evangelina's heart jumped. How many years had it been since she stood awkwardly in the YMCA's multipurpose room preparing for her first yoga class? How many years since that day she had first seen Rose? Six years? Yes, Evangelina thought, it had been six long years, but she still knew a sun salutation when she saw it and she still missed Rose.

"*Surya Namaskar.* Sun Salutation," the yoga instructor Rayne Forrest said that very first day. "Repeat after me, *Surya Namaskar.* For the next six weeks, you will learn and practice Sun Salutation not just here but at home as you begin your every morning."

"Yeah, right!" thought Evangelina who had no plans to practice a second more than needed to make herself look competent in class. She already didn't like Rayne Forrest because of her hokey name, which Evangelina suspected had been invented to go with her yoga expert persona, and because she found Rayne's voice cloying and was not inclined to trust it.

Still, Evangelina stood barefoot on her borrowed blue mat in the YMCA's drab multipurpose room. Not even the six sandalwood incense burners could overpower the pool chlorine, and the mandala-print fabric over the windows was not enough to transform the room into a believable yoga studio, though she did give Rayne points for trying. What was she even doing here, Evangelina wondered. But here she was and it was too late to leave.

Evangelina had chosen to stand in the third row, the back row, to the far right, which was, she felt, the ideal spot for her, the oddity in the room. Feeling like an oddity was not uncommon for Evangelina, but it was uncomfortable. The other nine women wore stretchy snug yoga pants, sports bras, and various colored tank tops. Some of the women were slender and well defined while others were on the heavy side with drooping upper arm flesh. For all their differences, the other women looked to Evangelina like they belonged not only in their clothes but also in their bodies, and this bothered Evangelina who felt her unbelonging as deeply as she knew she must look it.

That morning Evangelina had pulled her gray sweatpants and Notre Dame t-shirt from the top of the laundry basket thinking clothing wouldn't matter, thinking that she was doing exactly what the instructions required: "Wear something comfortable you can move in." Evangelina had been comfortable enough in her clothes when she put them on at home, but now that she was standing barefoot on her borrowed blue mat in the YMCA multipurpose room, she felt uncomfortably different—maybe inferior, maybe superior, maybe some of both.

"Whatever," Evangelina shrugged. She'd had no reason to spend money on a new yoga outfit when yoga hadn't even been her idea but Russell's who had stumbled upon the sexy yoga YouTube channel one night long after Evangelina had fallen asleep and decided what Evangelina needed for her birthday was this.

Sexy yoga. The name alone made Evangelina feel degraded, especially when Russell said it. Even she who knew nothing of yoga knew that sexy was not yoga's aim.

In the park, Evangelina watched the woman fold forward, bending slightly at the knees, her fingertips touching her toes. She remembered how Rose's fingertips had touched her toes, how each of Rose's digits had worn its skin so perfectly. Though Evangelina would later tell Russell and anybody who would listen that she had only noticed Rose because Rose was in her direct line of vision one row ahead and one position to the left, Evangelina knew she was lying, but she didn't know how to speak the truth to others let alone herself.

In truth, Evangelina had been drawn to the whole of Rose from her elegantly long fingers and shapely toes, to her bruise-colored birthmark resting like a ripe plum on her right shoulder, to her perfect abundance of flesh and curve and muscle. Evangelina had been drawn to how Rose gave herself over to each asana as though her body would not fail her, as though her confidence were perfection, as though her inhale and exhale were the universe. As Evangelina watched Rose move through the asanas of her first sun salutation, she was filled with a deep longing, and though her mind told her she was being weird, maybe even obsessive, she could not stop her heart from pulling toward this stranger who would soon become her dearest friend.

Friend. She remembered the two of them calling each other friend so many times over the nine months they were together right up to the two of them standing in Rose's driveway with the new "Sold!" sign planted in the grass beside them like a weed that didn't belong or maybe more like a tombstone.

"I love you," Rose said as Evangelina held on to her, memorizing what it felt like to have their arms wrapped around each other, to have Rose's breasts pressed firmly against hers, inhaling the cherry scent of Rose's freshly washed hair.

"I love you too," Evangelina said, tears spilling down her face. "I wish you didn't have to move. I've never had a friend like you." Even as Evangelina said "friend," she knew she was lying, knew that friend was not all that Rose was. What she felt was that Rose was her soul mate, but she didn't know how to say that, and it scared her to even think that this was what she felt toward this woman who had broken down all her defenses, all her defenses but the most guarded defense of them all.

"I know," Rose said, lifting Evangelina's face and wiping her tears with her thumb. "I wish I didn't have to leave you. I won't miss anything about Indiana, but I will miss you. I will miss you so much I would almost stay just for you, but I can't." And then Rose brightened, "Come with me? You could, you know, if you wanted."

Evangelina flooded with want. She wanted to pack up and leave right then, wanted to move with Rose to Canada, start a new life with someone with whom every conversation, laugh, adventure, and hug filled her with joy and made her come alive in her own skin. Standing in Rose's driveway, Evangelina remembered back to May when they'd driven through Amish country out by Nappanee when the world was aflame with bloom and color, when the air smelled sweet of cows and blossoms and grass and recent rains, when the earth was alive and her soul was too as she and Rose pointed out to each other their favorite farmhouses, which were always the ones with the wraparound porches. She remembered Rose shouting out, "That's it! That's it! Stop the car and go back!" so Evangelina had stopped the car, reversed, and backed up in front of the house that had so caught Rose's attention, an Amish farmhouse with a covered porch wrapped around three of the four sides. "This is perfect," Rose had gasped, grabbing Evangelina's hand. "I would live here with you!"

In the yard, Amish girls with bonneted heads ran barefoot through the green grass, their blue dresses flowing out around them. When the girls saw their car stop, they turned and looked toward them, still smiling. Evangelina smiled back and waved with the hand Rose wasn't holding, wanting both to stay and drive quickly away. She couldn't bring herself to turn and look at Rose for all the gears in Evangelina's brain had jammed when she'd told her body she couldn't feel what she felt, which was feeling that she wanted to kiss Rose and then to tumble headlong into a new imagined life, but she couldn't. She was married to Russell. She couldn't because she didn't have a name for what she wanted but she knew that what she wanted couldn't be what she'd always been told it was.

What she wanted was Rose, love, and a life with somebody she became herself around. What she had felt just seconds before was exhilarating freedom, an opening, and an escape from the unhappiness she had never been able to fully articulate for herself, but then she'd met Rose who listened to her and loved her exactly as she was, and she thought maybe this and not what she had with Russell was love.

But how could she leave the life she knew? How would she explain it? And wouldn't she in the end come to ruin as her father had always said happened to homosexuals? "I know what you are," Evangelina remembered her father telling her when she was twelve, when her world was falling apart after her best friend Sue, her only friend, moved away to Maine with her family to trap and sell lobsters, a life Evangelina couldn't have, a life she didn't even want, wanting only Sue by her side to keep writing stories and drawing pictures together and to talk about what it was like to both be weird in the world. "I know what you are," Evangelina's father had said, but he never said what that was, maybe he couldn't even say it, so all Evangelina heard was *bad* and *too much* and *crazy* and *sinful*. She couldn't live as herself in her father's world, and she knew without him ever saying *homosexual,* without him ever saying *lesbian,* that these were the words he could not say, the words she'd heard him reserve for the people he most despised.

"I'd live there with you," Evangelina had said in front of the Amish house with the wraparound porch, and then, so afraid of what she felt, she had added, "just as friends, of course."

"Does it matter what we call it?" Rose asked, leaning over to kiss Evangelina on the cheek. "I just want to live with you."

Outside the Amish girls had run off again, out toward the garden where their mother was planting seeds. Evangelina envied how carefree they looked, no matter how they may have felt on the inside, knowing for herself that people, even the Amish, were always more than they appeared.

Evangelina let go of Rose's hand, having released the just-as-friends safety valve she had always relied on and that she couldn't take back now. What she felt in the driveway was the forward motion of her feelings stopped again, keeping herself from being propelled into so many unspoken and unrealized futures, keeping herself safe when what she wanted, what she needed, was not to be safe but to be saved. Evangelina knew not even Rose could save her but that she could save herself and had once again chosen not to.

Evangelina focused her attention again on the woman in the park now in perfect plank position. She tried to remember what it had been like to be in such perfect balance—shoulders above wrists, back straight, lungs exhaling every bit of air she held inside herself. She remembered it was good. She remembered feeling good in both her body and her mind, remembered expressing this to Rose and through yoga, which she practiced faithfully for nine months, long after the YMCA class ended, having quit only when Rose moved to Canada. She remembered feeling like she belonged in her own skin, and she missed that.

Evangelina turned away from the woman in the park, from the sun salutation half-way through, the woman's body now lowered to the ground, ready for her next exhale.

But that was six years ago, six years of holding everything close, especially this pain she felt, for to exhale her pain would be too great a risk, and what would come next if she let it out? So Evangelina held her pain close, buried it under layers of busyness, for this was her way and surely easier than expression, easier than change.

Evangelina Empties the Washer

At the end of the wash cycle, after Evangelina had removed from the washer two armloads of blankets, towels, assorted underwear and socks, she looked down into the shiny metal drum and saw still clinging to the sides one striped orange-and-white sock and one ragged, red-checkered dishcloth, clinging in the way she had once clung to the wall of the Gravitron at the county fair when she was thirteen and the best thing in life was to enter the Gravitron and let it spin her around and around and around, reaching for her cousin Jo's hand and holding it tight at the starting sound of the crunch and whir of the gears preparing to drop the bottom and leave them hanging impossibly with nothing to stand on, the floor several feet below, and it was this impossible thing she was doing—every single time, this most impossible thing—that thrilled her, stuck there as she was to the inside of the Gravitron and going faster and faster and faster until finally she was all spun out and the grin of terror plastered on her face began to relax as the spin began to slow, Evangelina feeling herself slowly slipping down the wall even as the gears started again, this time raising the floor back to where it would meet her feet, and though Evangelina didn't want this ride, this feeling, to end, never wanted it to end, still it always did and she would think in her head, "See, that wasn't so bad, was it?" even as Jo would say, "Let's go again, Eva! There's no line, just us," and so again they would go, just the two of them, this time Evangelina spreading her arms and legs wide like a jumping jack, daring the Gravitron, this force greater than herself, to whirl her into rapture on the Gravitron's terms but with her chosen posture.

Evangelina Watches Cockroaches

It did not take much to make Evangelina feel uncomfortable. All it took were bodies. Any bodies. Human bodies, cat bodies, kangaroo bodies, toad bodies. Even long brown cockroach bodies with their bottoms smashing up against one another and their heads facing in opposite directions as their antennae waggled wildly, motions of thrusting, of sliding their hard cockroach shells back and forth and making (she imagined, for her hearing was not in fact so acute) a most unpleasant noise like overlong fingernails softly clacking and clicking against each other in a slidey sort of way, heat building up from the necessary friction of undiluted cockroach sex so that she wondered if a spark might ignite and the two earnest roaches might spontaneously combust.

Watching cockroaches mate at 4:33 a.m. on top of her cousin Jo's bedroom dresser was not how Evangelina had planned to spend her first night or, in fact, any of her six planned mid-July vacation nights in Wilmington, North Carolina, and while her plan to sleep through the night had seemed in her mind a reasonable one, she did not always get to choose how things went. In fact, Evangelina recognized, she rarely got to choose or rather, after choosing, she rarely got to experience events as the gradually unfolding and well-orchestrated plan in her sometimes particular and always, she was certain, reasonable mind.

In truth, Evangelina had not awoken at 4:29 with any intention of watching cockroaches. Indeed, she had had no idea there would be any cockroaches to watch. Evangelina had awoken feeling a familiar biological need, the urgency of which she measured by pressing her palms down firmly against her nightgowned abdomen. Evangelina sighed at the inconvenience even as she recognized it as routine and anticipated, something to get up and take care of before returning to sleep as she always did at home. She pulled back the lightweight yet remarkably warm down comforter, which contrasted nicely with the immediacy of cool satin sheets that felt smooth and fluid against her legs, like water in her Uncle Don's calm and quiet pond where she once swam as a girl with Jo.

Or, rather, Jo swam, her tanned and muscled arms slicing the surface of the water in strong certain strokes across the pond and back again like she owned it. Evangelina was content to lie on her back on the water's surface and drift—just drift—surrendering her body to the wedded motions of the wind and the water, relishing liquid coolness against her back, the scorch of late morning sun upon her front from forehead to toe tips and everything—even her newly sprouted buds of breasts covered discreetly with black Lycra—in between. Why was it then that she had stopped going to the pond? Evangelina couldn't recall, but what did it matter, really, when any remembrance could only ever be half-dream, half-real?

There was to Jo's guest bed an ease and a comfort that Evangelina liked. She couldn't have quite said why, though for one thing Russell was not in it, nor in fact was he closer than a two-day's drive away. And for another, Jo had made up the guest bed with Evangelina's sleeping comfort in mind.

This, Evangelina thought, was both a great kindness and a luxury. Evangelina closed her eyes, sighed, lay still, and spread her body to mimic how she once had floated on Uncle Don's pond—arms outstretched in a T, legs splayed out in a V. When she closed her eyes Evangelina could feel herself floating and the satin felt cool like water against sun-scorched skin, but she could not in the end ignore the urge in her bladder.

Before leaving Evangelina for the night, Jo had turned on a nightlight made from a conch shell the size of a softball in the outlet between the dresser and the door. Evangelina reasoned, before dismissing herself as silly, that she was three years younger and Jo still thought of her as a child afraid of the dark. This light was a strange thing, Evangelina thought, because for a nightlight it was enormous, but for a conch shell it was quite small. When Jo had plugged in the electrified conch, Evangelina had felt an impulse to unplug the shell and hold it to her ear so she could hear the ocean the way she had as a child with the conch her father had purchased at the St. Vincent DePaul's in South Bend on his way home from work. Evangelina's hands had been small and smooth, being only six and in the first grade, and she had at first been scared by how rough the ridges felt against her smooth hands. How curious it had looked, something between a tower turret and the pale concrete sculpture of a hedgehog she had once liked but her mother had not purchased at Garden's Treasures, the concrete gallery where her mother bought drab gray gnomes she liked to paint bright colors and then set up in her herb garden as guardians.

Evangelina remembered this moment with her first conch the way she remembered those moments adrift on Uncle Don's pond when gray clouds would cover the sun and her body would chill and she would close her eyes and wait for the clouds to move on and for her godmother sun to return to warm her pale, freckled flesh and flood her eyes through their delicate lids with heat and light and sparks and flashes as though the lightning bolts inside her brain had been made visible at last. Curious, Evangelina had felt more than thought as she now held in her hands this shell that could never have come from her uncle's pond but that belonged to somewhere, some other water body she couldn't begin to fathom the breadth of. Curious. Like nothing one should ever grow to love, yet she did.

Because her mother had told her that a soft sea creature had once lived inside this wondrous shell of a home, Evangelina had longed to know whatever could have made a soft sea creature leave, so she asked but her mother had only said in a voice that sounded cramped and tired to Evangelina, "I don't know, Evie. Maybe the creature became too large for her shell, posted a 'to rent' sign and moved on?" and her father could only say, "You know, conch meat tastes delicious, like clams, they say, but I've never tried it," which came nowhere near answering her question. Only when Evangelina showed the conch to Jo on a Thursday after school did she learn what she hadn't known, what she needed to know.

"The ocean's in there, Eva. Listen," Jo said, holding the inner folds of the conch against the outer folds of Evangelina's ear, the feeling of shell on flesh so cool and smooth she closed her eyes to hear blossoming outward from deep within the roar of a distant but certain ocean. "Here," Jo said. "You hold it now," and so Evangelina took the shell in her own hands and cradled it against her own ear, not quite trusting that the ocean's roar would continue, but it did. For as long as she held the conch to her ear, the sound went on and on and on until she knew she could always trust the ocean to be there for her. Now, standing in Jo's guest bedroom at 4:30 a.m. on a hot July night, it struck Evangelina as sad but also necessary that the soft sea creature had to leave its home, which had now for whatever reason she couldn't fully comprehend become a glowing nightlight. And then she thought that had the soft sea creature never left, there could never have been an ocean within the shell for her to hear.

Evangelina did not unplug the conch—whatever would Jo have thought had she walked in to see Evangelina holding the nightlight up to her ear, listening—but her fingers remembered tracing the ridges, bumps, scars, and spiraled turrets of the conch with her child's fingers until she reached the underside where everything changed and the rough gave way to smooth, curve, and a leaning inward as she trusted herself to feel beyond the creamy white blooming into bubblegum-pink, bubblegum-pink darkening into shadow that she could see with her eyes, her fingers slipping deep and deeper into some grand mystery. Smooth.

Smooth the way Jo's body sliced the surface of her father's pond before diving folded-palms first below the surface and disappearing, Jo's long strong feet the last thing Evangelina, upright and treading water, could see, and she was breathless to see where and when her sea monster cousin would reappear, and bracing for whether this time—this time!—she would feel against her slender hips the sudden pressure and pull of Jo's hands and before she could even think to struggle to be pulled deep, deep below the surface where she could pretend she too had been cursed to be a sea monster like Jo, but knowing always that she would surface and this time with Jo beside her, the two of them laughing so hard all they could in the end do was toss themselves back against the surface of the water and laugh and drift and rest and scan the clouds for whatever kingdoms and creatures they could spy, Evangelina saying, "I wish you wouldn't pull me under like that. I could drown, you know." And all Jo could do was grin and say, "Then you'd better take a deep breath before I do, Eva," as if she could ever have been as prepared as that. As if she would have wanted to be.

With the conch nightlight's glow to guide her, Evangelina slid out from the comfort of her newly claimed satiny sea, the air around her cool and air-conditioned dry. Jo's bathroom wasn't far—down the hall two doors and around the corner by the entrance to the kitchen—but while Evangelina could navigate her own home without seeing, trusting her hands, her feet, her body to know the corners, walls, and furniture, this she knew she could not do at Jo's and so, six steps forward, she reached the dresser where she could see the outline of her upturned glasses looking like a double-yolk egg or twin moons, should there be such a wonder in the sky, and this made her think about the tides and how two moons might affect the ocean. And then, as Evangelina reached for her glasses, she saw through her own lenses a monstrous scuttle of what seemed a double-bodied alien creature, which gave her sudden and absolute pause, her motion resuming only when she, with quiet caution, pulled the small chain of the green banker's lamp and illuminated cockroach coitus.

Though she would have anticipated, hoped even, for the light to interrupt the insects' fervent reproductive endeavor, if the light and her all-seeing presence had any impact whatsoever, it was only to intensify cockroach coupling.

Or perhaps, and Evangelina reasoned that this was most likely the case, their behavior remained unchanged while the clarity of the act in which these insects of the night were engaged became all the clearer to Evangelina who could not now keep from watching them, watching especially the small one's antennae waggling as if in great distress.

Keeping her hand to the far side of the cockroaches, Evangelina slid her glasses from the top of Jo's dresser and centered them securely on the bridge of her nose, tucking the frames behind her ears, all the while watching as the cockroaches sharpened into focus, exchanging their initial monstrousness for a monstrous curiosity that settled deep in Evangelina just below her breastbone. That these two creatures joined as one, no less than five inches in their mutual merry-making length, both horrified and fascinated Evangelina. Not that Evangelina would ever admit this, not even to Jo for whom she would spin this nocturnal encounter of beetle lust into a casual tale were she to mention it at all. Of necessity her digested story would, Evangelina knew, still hold a shadow of disgust and trauma for the sake of sympathy and storytelling but she never would, never could, own up to her sudden desire to either flee her skin or crush these hard bodies with the soles of Jo's even harder Doc Martens.

So it was that Evangelina stood at the corner of her cousin Jo's guest room dresser in Wilmington, North Carolina, watching cockroaches mate on her cousin Jo's dresser, realizing as she watched that all the verbs she had ever connected to the movements of beetle-type insects came suddenly into her mind. Cockroaches *did* waggle antennae. Cockroaches *did* scuttle across hard surfaces. Cockroaches *did* cock their heads at odd angles and even more so when they were doing it together as a double-bodied unit. Cockroaches *did* (she was certain, though she had not tested this theory and was not yet certain whether she would) crunch when hard and heavy objects like Jo's Doc Martens were smashed down upon their waggling, scuttling, cock-headed bodies. *Waggle, scuttle, cock, crunch. Waggle, scuttle, cock, crunch.*

As the cockroaches moved mysteriously in unison yet also in opposition, Evangelina noted how the smaller of the two appeared to be struggling to scuttle away from the larger cockroach but couldn't, held fast like her hindquarters were glued somehow to his with glue that she presumed he owned the bottle of, given his own steady concentration and lack of distress. Evangelina turned away. A nasty trick. A cruel game. The cockroach equivalent of Derek slipping something into Karen's rum and coke when Karen had only gone to Derek's after-prom party wanting a drink and a good time, which to Karen had meant being held in Derek's arms and maybe a kiss or three but that was all.

Evangelina couldn't go there. Couldn't but knew she was already back there sitting with Karen in her grandmother's avocado-green Oldsmobile '98 when everybody but the two of them had gone home after Derek and Pastor Rod's "Growing in God" talk about young men and how visual they are and about young women and how modest they need to be because men, men were created to not be able to help themselves because somehow that was a part of God's design and Karen—sweet, kind Karen with a laugh like a tornado that touched down on the fields of her heart sometimes—sitting in the driver's seat with the key in the ignition unturned, just spilling out everything she had kept bottled up about Derek and prom from a week before, everything Karen remembered being a blank in her mind but still her body remembered pain in places she'd never even touched before, her body remembered blood—hers—and semen—his—and Karen felt that this must have been her fault, been all her fault because that prom dress she'd chosen, she knew now her dad had been right about how low-cut it was and how she shouldn't have worn it to prom, though when she chose her dress she thought it made her look pretty, that's all, just pretty the way it rested on her and the way her body filled it, but going to Derek's after-prom party at all, wasn't that just leading him on? And now no man would want her for a wife because she wasn't pure and she had sinned but she hadn't meant to sin, hadn't meant to be impure, and when she had woken up she was all alone in Derek's dark bedroom hearing voices and music and the party downstairs, but she just stared up at a ceiling covered in glow-in-the-dark stars that Derek should have been too old for but clearly wasn't, and wanted more than anything to be outside under the blaze of real stars where one might fall and burn all the way to the ground and into her body there for the taking, burn her up once and for all because whether it was punishment or forgiveness or sympathy she deserved, Karen was certain being burned to ash by a falling star would do the trick, even the score, eliminate the feeling, the problem, the everything that was her and that was wrong, and God, He could have stopped Derek but He didn't so maybe all this was meant to teach her a lesson, teach her what it meant to be a godly woman.

Evangelina had shuffled through her feelings like a deck of cards, shuffled and reshuffled, unsure which feeling to choose, which one would choose her, showing nothing of the ache she felt deep inside for Karen and somehow, too, for her own self. Evangelina hadn't gone to Derek's party. She hadn't even gone to prom. The whole idea of prom and parties had always seemed pointless and painful not because she couldn't get a date but because she never wanted one, never wanted a boyfriend either. Maybe if Evangelina had just made an effort she could have gone to prom for Karen, for her friend, but she hadn't and because she hadn't gone she hadn't protected her friend and because she hadn't protected her friend there had been Derek and . . .

Evangelina had so wished she could settle on a feeling just so she could have stopped not knowing what to say, what to do, how to feel, but she couldn't. She remembered Karen's eyes, a wild tangle of lostness, hurt, and beauty, remembered Karen's tear-streaked face and Karen's sweet voice cracking even as Karen begged to know, "Am I bad, Eva? I'm bad, aren't I? Please tell me I'm not bad, Eva," and Evangelina had no words to say but only thoughts of badness, her own badness with her own body, and her own badness with how she had never wanted any body but her own but now felt in her arms the shudder of Karen collapsing into sobs and she held tight hoping she could somehow keep together all the pieces of her friend exploding outward now, all the pieces of herself imploding inward as she always did, as even then she knew she must do. As for Derek, Evangelina had wanted to smash him, wanted to smash him even now. Smash him like a cockroach. That much she remained certain of, sudden rage the ace of spades in her deck.

Evangelina watched the smaller cockroach lunge forward, then slip backwards again and again and every time, stuck, and she felt in her brow a tightness she knew must have been there since the memory of Karen had crossed her mind. Evangelina willed herself to relax her face, loosen her brow, lift her eyes, and force a smile, which she hoped would lessen the sudden slash of memory, but it didn't, couldn't, and so she thought of Karen as Karen was now—mild Karen, careful Karen, door-to-door evangelizing Karen, quiver-full-of-kids Karen, husband-adoring Karen—how completely Karen had been able to take (had had to take?) cold, calculating, incapacitating rape and turn it into something that looked like the appearance of love, the falling star she had hoped would burn her up having burned itself out in space as she watched and so she had wished on it the only way she knew how, which was in the life she ended up getting for herself. A half-life, Evangelina sometimes thought, because when she saw Karen from time to time there never was a tornado in her laugh anymore, nor even a true laugh, just an occasional nervous chuckle, but Evangelina never told her friend she missed that about her or even that she noticed her laugh had gone missing, just asked how her life was and wished her well. It seemed to Evangelina that somehow they'd both gotten lost along the way but differently, and maybe Karen's lostness was really no worse than her own, no worse than the sadness she sometimes felt in her own life when she let herself feel anything at all, still finding it hard to settle on a feeling when she shuffled the cards, most of the time leaving the deck untouched in the top bureau drawer, the queen of hearts gone missing long ago.

Antennae waggling, the cockroaches scuttled, cocked their heads, looked up at Evangelina then back down to the dresser. That Jo called these turd-colored insects "palmetto bugs" made no difference to Evangelina and, in fact, her cousin's designation irked her. These were still, plain and simple, cockroaches, though Evangelina had wisely, she believed, kept this fact to herself. Evangelina knew she was right because she had googled "PALMETTO BUGS COCKROACHES SAME DIFFERENT" and discovered not only on Wikipedia but also on the more authoritative Orkin.com that no matter what a Southerner might choose to call them (palmetto bug sounding practically pleasant, tropical, even a touch exotic in a Hawaiian sort of way) these long-bodied, short-legged, brown bugs really were just plain old "American cockroaches," a nationalistic designation that likewise bothered Evangelina, sounding practically patriotic, which irked her because designating a filthy cockroach as "American" seemed an affront to her American way of life. Evangelina was distracting herself and as soon as she knew it, she couldn't continue, heading straight back into the abyss that was cockroach sex playing out on the dresser in front of her.

Evangelina didn't want to keep watching, but she could not bring herself to turn away. The way they had backed up into each other, each looking in an opposite direction, was curious to Evangelina—why else should she keep returning to it? So she thought about this arrangement, this body-to-body reproductive connection not only with no eye contact but with distinctly different outlooks, the larger cockroach's vision dominated by the giant E of Jo's value-sized Excedrin bottle, the smaller cockroach at the very edge of the dresser looking out over the precipice where what waited below was a cardboard box spilling over with Reader's Digest Condensed books, a cockroach paradise if only it could be reached, Evangelina knew, but did the cockroach? She wondered, and in wondering lowered her head toward the dresser just enough to approximate the cockroach's vision, just enough to know that this cockroach could not see beyond its vast and unknown openness. Evangelina wondered if cockroaches even knew about gravity. Looking at the roach's body, she could see it had something like wings. But could cockroaches fly? She didn't know.

The movement of exoskeleton against exoskeleton made Evangelina think of plate tectonics and the ancient history of the Earth, her knowledge of which was slight but certain, and she had what she recognized as a curious moment of imagining a PBS *Nature* documentary where the sound of the mating cockroaches could have been amplified a thousand times and thus been so jarring and severe her eardrums wouldn't have been able to handle the dissonance. Hadn't she read somewhere, heard somewhere, watched somewhere that cockroaches fondled each other's antennae to determine the sex of a potential mate? Evangelina wondered if that was anything like handholding. She wondered what the difference would feel like and whether mistakes were ever made or if mistakes were really mistakes anyway. Cockroaches, she thought, didn't have brains, or was that just another insect stereotype? Who determined that in the first place? Instinct. Ruled by instinct.

Instinct was all there was to cockroaches, wasn't it? No thought or conscious decision making, just urge beyond reason—urge to mate, urge to reproduce, every bit of them honed in these moments for this purpose, so much so that as she stood there she imagined herself to have sprayed at them a whole can of roach killer, every drop of poison released, and the cockroaches still working and working and working against all odds at what her father had so clinically called the "biological imperative," a phrase she had never forgotten and one that had not served her well in her rudimentary eighth-grade sex education class. But if urge was all there was, then why the need for glue? Then why the smaller cockroach's struggle to escape?

Evangelina thought again of cockroach brains, of the idea that they had no brains, only instinct and impulse and urge, of biological imperative driving the only things that mattered to these creatures that sometimes were said to be driven to dominate the Earth, that could spill out babies upon babies upon babies until, left to their own devices, Jo's dresser and walls and floors and ceiling would be covered with them. Covered. Roach babies and adults and more mating roaches everywhere, covering everything, so thick and solid and patterned against the wall that one would think it wasn't at all the roaches moving but only the few bare patches of rose-patterned wallpaper that were on the move. And even then the roaches would be eating the wallpaper, leaving behind what?

Everything living had to have a brain, didn't it? Every living animal at least, and as much as Evangelina didn't care for cockroaches in the slightest, as much as disgust filled her very being as she stood there watching, unable to tear herself away from watching, even she had to admit that cockroaches were an animal made to walk the earth and populate it. Biological imperative. The thought of Karen and Derek. The ace of spades pulled again from the deck and she shuffling to feel something different than rage, something smaller, something numbered at a four or below.

When she had first arrived at Jo's house, a cockroach ("Palmetto bug," her cousin had called it with a hint of Southern pride) lounged on the top cement step by the front door as though waiting to be let in, its long antennae waggling at her in welcome, or was it threat, or was it even just cockroaches doing what they did with neither welcome nor threat but just—just what?—didn't everything have to mean something? Evangelina hadn't known. Evangelina had reached over and rang the doorbell and waited, poking the roach with her shoe and being surprised at its unwillingness to scuttle off elsewhere. Maybe the cockroach was sick. It didn't look sick, but then how would she know? Maybe the cockroach was bold? This she thought was more likely as the only difference being poked had made was that the cockroach waggled its antennae more vigorously, shifted itself and did a half-turn without going anywhere, resolute, Evangelina thought, in holding its ground.

"Coming!" Jo had called out from inside the house, her voice certain and full as it had been since childhood, as her sandaled footfalls grew louder with each approaching step. There was, as there always had been, Evangelina remembered, a weight to Jo's being that commanded attention, and maybe this was why Evangelina had finally driven out of Indiana and through four states to reach this town at the edge of the Atlantic Ocean, so different from where they had both grown up, this place her cousin had claimed as home. "How the hell are you, cuz?" Jo asked, throwing open the white screen door and throwing her arms wide. Evangelina just stood there feeling suddenly stiff and uncertain, then looked down to find that the cockroach was no longer there, having been either scared off the porch or welcomed inside, Evangelina didn't exactly know which.

Again, the feeling of hands on hips. Again, the feeling of being pulled underwater. Again, becoming a sea monster but this time for real, inside a shell where a soft sea creature had once lived but had left to find a bigger home, or maybe had been eaten—she never did know—the shell now salty ocean-filled and carpeted with white sand that glimmered like stars fallen from the sky long ago that had found a place to rest.

Evangelina could not help but feel in herself that this loudness, this fullness, this embarrassingly present presence, this ocean roar, was how things always were, always had been with Jo, even as Jo grabbed her up and squeezed her in her strong arms, squeezed Evangelina so tight she felt like a grape being pressed for wine, or rather like a withered grape caught in the press that had nothing left to give, no matter how much someone might try and love her into wine. So she just stayed still, waiting for Jo's release, even as she longed to be pulled beneath the surface again.

"Goodness, Jo!"

I wish you wouldn't pull me under like that. I could drown, you know.

Jo threw back her head and laughed a laugh that surely would have sent scuttling even the largest and most persistent cockroach. "Breathe, Eva," Jo laughed, clapping Evangelina on her back. "Just breathe, and later we'll go for a swim. But first, get yourself on in here! I've been waiting so long for you to arrive."

Evangelina Dreams a Dream

And so it was that Evangelina found herself at the outer limits of a town called Hicksville, and she knew it to be Hicksville because the sign read "Welcome to Hicksville!" in dark deep letters burned into pale wood, and Evangelina knew she was in Hicksville though where she wanted to be was somewhere else, somewhere further away but not too far away, a city that had a zoo with otters, a botanical conservatory with a desert, and a library with so many books it took up a whole city block, and that the place where she wanted to be was Fort Wayne because she had once been to Fort Wayne to visit her mother's sister, and because she had once spent a day in Fort Wayne with Rose, but here she was in Hicksville instead.

And so it was that Evangelina walked through a town called Hicksville looking for dolphins at the end of Main Street, because dolphins lived in and swam in the ocean that dead-ended Main Street as if this ocean and these dolphins had every reason to exist, or more that they needed no reason to exist because living was itself enough, no reason required.

And so it was that Evangelina saw dolphins just beyond her reach, but still, they were there bounding through the waves, the waves looking real and sounding real, the crashing of waves so full in her ears and so close to the buildings of Hicksville that surely the ocean must now be at full tide, but just as the waves were at first so real, now they looked to Evangelina realer than real and so not real at all but more like cutouts from an ancient map of the sort where sea monsters lived at the edges, and Evangelina wanted for there to be in the ocean at the edge of Hicksville sea monsters with long necks, flashy-scaled bodies, burning red eyes, and diamond teeth revealing them to be the beautiful monsters they really were, and she wanted to be devoured, swallowed up, swallowed down, wanted to sleep in the sea monster's cavernous belly just waiting to be, to be, to be, and that's what she wanted, because the waves looked like they deserved sea monsters but there were only dolphins leaping and bounding closer and closer to shore, closer and closer to her.

And so it was that Evangelina felt herself feeling sad somehow even as she saw further out into the ocean where shapes that were dolphins or maybe could just as well have been whales swam and dived and surfaced over and over, and Evangelina knew she couldn't know for certain whether the creatures were dolphins or whales, and she knew she couldn't know because this was her within a dream with her thinking in it, but there was something there, something about the dolphins that she was supposed to know or learn only she didn't know what that was, didn't know what ever she could do as she couldn't touch the dolphins close to shore any more than she could touch those further out, couldn't swim with them, and the ocean, well, maybe that ocean wasn't real either but cardboard cutouts with the waves so severe, caricatures of themselves so that they couldn't drown her, couldn't drown her but could maybe fall on her and cut her as though they were made out of paper, yes paper, she thought.

And so it was that Evangelina turned away, away from the ocean and the dolphins, turned back to look at the storefronts of Hicksville only one of which mattered to her, that one having the words "Bubble Tea" painted in bright blue across the glass window so Evangelina stepped inside only to find herself staring at wall-to-wall chalkboards on which were written every flavor of bubble tea her mind could contain, every flavor, which included but was not limited to almond-taro-milk-coconut-strawberry-kiwi-green-matcha-and-on-and-on-and-on, but there was only one bubble tea Evangelina wanted and that was the original milk tea with black boba, black, round, slippery, chewy boba, and she wanted it because that was all she had ever wanted or, no, not all she had ever wanted but all she wanted in that moment and in no other moment, in that moment that was now, bubble tea was all she knew to want and so that is what Evangelina ordered or must have ordered because she heard herself say *original milk tea with black boba please* and then she held the drink in her hands and she drank it up through the straw and she was pleased, no longer caring that Hicksville was where she was because she had found in Hicksville the best bubble tea shop in the world called, quite simply, "Bubble Tea."

And so it was that Evangelina found herself to be walking again, feeling something that she thought maybe was happy but not knowing whether happy was to be trusted when she had never been able to trust it before, but when she just stood in the sunshine drinking down her bubble tea so cold and sweet and creamy, the boba so soft and chewy and tasting a little earthy, a little malty, when she stood just drinking, liking the taste and feel of boba on her tongue and between her teeth and then sliding, sliding, sliding all the way down what her mother used to call her gullet like the gullet of a bird, like Evangelina herself was just some bird with a gullet but Evangelina knew she wasn't a bird at all, knew she had no wings, no flight in her, though maybe she had swim and scales and gills, yes, gills and not a gullet, which maybe was why there was an ocean here in Hicksville and she was drawn to it, and then Evangelina felt happy.

And so it was that as Evangelina felt herself to be happy drinking bubble tea on a sidewalk in Hicksville, the sun slipped behind clouds as dark as the sidewalk and Evangelina looked first up and then down, and the sidewalk that had seemed a gray expanse gave way to a shimmer that was more than color, a shimmer that was a movement of sparks that to the untrained eye looked like sparkles but weren't, that existed, moved, and shimmered without sunlight as there now was no sunlight shining down and Evangelina knew, just knew without having to be told (and who was there in this town to tell her anyway?) that this was an alternate universe, that all she had to do was step inside the shimmer and everything would be different, different not like better or worse but just *different*, and she felt so hungry just then for different that she stepped inside the shimmer of sidewalk.

And so it was that Evangelina, inside this alternate universe, was not sure she felt any different but felt more like she was waiting, just waiting as the dolphins swam in the ocean and as she stood inside this shimmering alternate universe when from the top of the tallest building in Hicksville, which was really only two stories tall, a man began to hurl anvils, boulders, and pianos that cracked and broke the sidewalk around Evangelina but not inside her shimmering alternate reality where the man's cartoon tools of destruction turned into brightly colored confetti and balloons that floated down but did not fall until they transformed into tricycles, red shiny tricycles with black bulb horns and chrome wheel covers—one of them at first, and then two, and then more—so pretty and shiny and looking so small until down they came crashing around her, crashing into the shimmer of her alternate universe so that now, now she had to dodge these beautiful child's things that were not at all child's things, being too large for a toddler or even a grown man to ride, being as tall as she was, her head level with the handlebars, and Evangelina wanted to stop them from falling though she was not afraid of the tricycles or of the man on the roof.

And so it was that Evangelina shouted up at the man on the roof in Hicksville to stop his throwing, shouted, *hey-stop-it-mister-you-could-hurt-someone* but still the tricycles kept dropping and all she could do was keep walking within this shimmering strip of an alternate reality where things really were different somehow, where the very promise of magic was made real in the concrete's shimmer, and so she did not want to step outside of it, even though this was not exactly where it was that she wanted to be, but still she had her bubble tea and she drank from the straw even as she walked within the shimmer to the end of the street where the dolphins swam, where maybe she could swim too.

And so it was that Evangelina walked on, for there was nothing she could do about the tricycles or the man on the roof, and though it didn't seem likely she would become a casualty, she still stepped aside when the tricycles fell and just kept walking, walking, walking in this alternate reality that already was somehow somewhere else, down the center of a street in a town called Hicksville where dolphins played at the outer limits and maybe sea monsters did too.

Evangelina Thinks About Teeth

The week before she started kindergarten, Evangelina's mother had told her family dentist Dr. Bob Robertson that she had been born with two teeth poking out from her upper gums, "like little beaver teeth," her mother had said, and Dr. Robertson, pulling back Evangelina's lips for one last look and running his fingers along her gum line had said, "Everything looks good. She was born to bite." Then they both laughed as Evangelina lay back in the chair with her mouth wide open, unable to speak.

Even as a child, the fact of her having been born with two fully formed teeth had struck Evangelina as something that set her apart from people who had begun their lives with smooth gums on both top and bottom the way babies are supposed to be born, the way her younger cousin Grant had been born. But not Evangelina, and this fact of having been born with two fully formed teeth had made her feel like she had a secret even if it was a secret that had never impacted her in any meaningful way.

When Evangelina thought now about her birth teeth, she brought to mind the picture she had seen on Facebook of an upper palate crowded with teeth and a caption that read, "This is what hyperdontia looks like!" Evangelina knew this picture had nothing to do with her having been born with teeth, but the image had branded itself upon her brain, persisting even after she checked Snopes and discovered the picture was a fake, which was to Evangelina both a relief and a disappointment. Yet it was only the picture that was fake, not hyperdontia itself, which was as real as the four extra molars in Freddy Mercury's mouth, and as real as the 232 supernumerary teeth removed from the jaw of that teenager Ashik Gavai in India.

Evangelina wondered about Ashik and his swollen jaw, about the teeth—denticles, the article had called them— that had been growing and multiplying undetected until the pain was so great that Ashik's father had driven him to Mumbai fearing the worst, fearing cancer, only to have a surgeon discover and remove 232 "little pearl-like teeth" from Ashik's lower jaw.

Nobody, Evangelina thought, needed that many teeth. It was enough for her to keep her own 32 teeth healthy and strong. Even harder to take in than the faked photo of the palate full of teeth was the real photo of Ashik's swollen face, and even harder to take in than that was the photo of the 232 extracted teeth arranged in a circular pattern, almost like a labyrinth, on green surgical cloth.

What must it feel like, Evangelina wondered, to have more teeth in a mouth than belong? She ran her tongue along both the outsides and the insides of her own jaw, first the bottom, then the top, and then over her hard palate. She liked starting her tongue at the back, curling her tongue backward to explore her soft palate above the uvula where the slide down into her throat began. She liked that her soft palate felt lightly textured with the tiniest of bumps, which reminded her of tastebuds even though they weren't. Just to be sure of this comparison, Evangelina folded her tongue over and rubbed her tongue against itself, liking the sandpapery tickle of it, but her tongue was not what concerned her so she returned the tip of her tongue as far back as she could extend it to her soft palate, then slowly slid her tongue forward onto her hard palate until she reached the ridges that came before the front teeth, the ridges that extended horizontally like speedbumps in the street in the housing development where she had once lived, the housing development where a toddler had once been hit by a speeding car and so in addition to the 10 MPH sign, the speedbumps had been added. That, Evangelina thought, had been a tragedy.

Evangelina wondered whether a mouthful of supernumerary teeth was a tragedy, a miracle, or maybe both. She thought it must be both, for how else would Ashik Gavai, an unknown teenager from the Indian countryside, become known around the globe through news outlets and dental journals and possibly even the Guinness Book of World Records? Why, he was known even to her in Elkhart, Indiana, a town whose only claim to dental fame was the tooth brick embedded with thousands of human teeth to memorialize a dentist's dog. But Evangelina knew sudden fame didn't make somebody a miracle, and it hadn't even been the boy who had become famous so much as his 232 extra teeth, Ashik's name mattering only insofar as it connected the world to the horrors of his jaw swollen with teeth he did not want, teeth that must have caused an ache of a magnitude she could not begin to comprehend. All Ashik had wanted, she was sure, was to be done with the pain and after that, she suspected, done with the notoriety that had made his pained face world famous for a day. That's all she would have wanted.

As Evangelina thought these things she continued to run her tongue over the speed bumps in her mouth. Bump,

bump, bump on the left. Bump, bump, bump on the right. And when she wanted a break from the speed bumps, she slid the tip of her tongue over the smooth path down the center as though her hard palate were a ribcage with a long smooth sternum down the center, the ribs being the speed bumps that slowed her tongue before they hit the back of her front teeth.

Compared to the boy with the 232 teeth, Evangelina's mouth was unremarkable, the uniqueness of having been born with two fully formed teeth having faded within months of her birth. She had no stories worth sharing—no root canals gone wrong, no teeth smashed out in childhood from bullies or playground accidents, not even any braces. Evangelina's teeth had always been straight, and what cavities she'd had were standard, the repairs undramatic, and clear sealant protected her from a multitude of sins.

Only once had anything gone even remotely wrong with Evangelina's teeth, and when things did, her mother saw that her teeth were promptly taken care of. When a stubborn baby tooth had refused to fall out, Dr. Robertson, who could be stubborn himself, had the good sense to refer her to a pediatric dental surgeon in Mishawaka, and her mother scheduled the first available appointment.

Dr. LuAnn Timothy, Evangelina had thought, was young and cool and knew what kids liked, and what kids liked was having a full array of handheld arcade games made to look like the stand-up originals at Aladdin's Castle in the Concord Mall. Dr. LuAnn, who had asked to be called by her first name, had all the games—Pac-Man, Ms. Pac-Man, Donkey Kong, Q-Bert, Frogger, Galaga, and Centipede— and of these Evangelina had chosen Ms. Pac-Man because on that day, sitting in Dr. LuAnn's examining chair, the power pellets had made her think of teeth, as though Ms. Pac-Man who had no teeth were trying to gain some for herself but they never stuck in her gums, just went down her gullet with the blinking blue ghosts. Not only was Dr. LuAnn young and cool, she was also a woman, a first for Evangelina who had never known a female doctor, who could hardly believe they existed.

Evangelina had found it reassuring that before Dr. LuAnn had even asked her to open her mouth, she had explained everything she would be doing and why each thing would be necessary. While Dr. Robertson had told Evangelina's mother her baby tooth had to come out, Dr. LuAnn explained that if her baby tooth didn't come out, there wouldn't be room for her permanent teeth to grow in straight, all of which made sense to Evangelina so that when Dr. LuAnn asked if she had any questions, she had none.

Before Novocaine had been injected into her upper gum, Dr. LuAnn said it would hurt, and before she put the mask on Evangelina's face, Dr. LuAnn told her she would be breathing sweet air, another name for nitrous oxide, and that it would make Evangelina feel relaxed, maybe even happy, but she would still be able to hear everything Dr. LuAnn and her hygienists would be saying and doing even though she wouldn't feel it in her mouth. If she did feel any pain, Dr. LuAnn had said, Evangelina was to tell them right away. When the Novocaine and sweet air were taking full effect, Dr. LuAnn asked for Ms. Pac-Man and Evangelina handed it to her to be put back on the shelf for the next child, the next child Evangelina wished would be her for she liked this dentist and her games and her manner. Then Evangelina closed her eyes and opened her mouth wide as instructed and she felt no fear.

Fading in and out of consciousness, Evangelina listened. She was aware of the sounds of tools against teeth and the feeling of pressure in her mouth, pressure which was not pain. She was aware of Dr. LuAnn and her hygienists talking not just about her and her tooth extraction, but also talking about the sweet air Evangelina had breathed as naturally as though it were oxygen but to a different effect, an effect she liked so much that as she listened to the talk around her—talk about staying after hours, about staying late just for fun and using the sweet air themselves—she wanted to be a part of that too because there was something about the smell of that sweet air and the feeling it produced of being aware but not aware in her body that made her understand how what they were talking about could be fun and also a relief from breathing normal air, but Evangelina knew she was too young to make such a choice for herself and she knew that such a choice was probably bad, wrong, immoral.

Evangelina knew her dad, who sometimes ranted about potheads, would have said so, but still she wanted this feeling not to end, for her to be able to feel again what she was feeling now for the first time but without her mouth wide open and her jaw padded with gauze, and without anybody—without even this woman dentist she liked and trusted—putting their hands and tools and drills inside her to extract a tooth that didn't want to leave. Only once did Evangelina feel something break, feel it and also hear it, a cracking sound, and she thought at first it was her tooth, but then Dr. LuAnn said, "Well, I'll be damned! That tool was brand new!" And Evangelina felt proud then because her baby tooth was strong and rooted and able to stay just where it was and break the tool designed to break her tooth.

But what about that boy? Evangelina wondered again. Surely they would have needed more than sweet air, surely they would have had to knock Ashik out completely, all the way out, unconscious out, to begin the extraction of all those tiny teeth, teeth like little pearls growing inside his jaw for no other reason than that they could, no other reason than that there was nothing to stop them.

Evangelina wished to feel a kinship with Ashik, but even she knew any kinship she could feel or imagine would be strained. Her greatest dental anomaly had been being born with two top teeth, and her toughest dental procedure had been the simple extraction of a baby tooth that didn't want to budge. It bothered her that she and Ashik had nothing more in common but try as she might Evangelina could not imagine having a jaw filled with 232 teeth let alone 232 teeth she didn't even know were there. She could more readily relate to the fake picture of the hard palate cluttered with teeth. She could imagine such chaos for she knew teeth were designed to tear and chew and break down food, to prepare it for digestion. Teeth, Evangelina thought, were so straightforward, meant to work in flawless tandem with the tongue as hers did. But what if instead of running her tongue over the smooth roof of her mouth she were to run her tongue over hundreds of teeth up where teeth should not be? Or what if her jaw were filled with teeth growing randomly, haphazardly, just waiting to spill out when a scalpel cut through her jaw?

This, like any notion of teeth being where teeth were not supposed to be, was both a horror and a fascination to Evangelina who had once spent a full half-hour imagining what her life would be like if she had a lower mandible growing out of her shoulder, teeth intact and sticking up.

How would she hide such a deformity from the world? Certainly, she wouldn't wear tank tops, but then she never wore them anyway. Shoulder pads, she suspected, absolutely ginormous shoulder pads, would have to be her solution. Better to be thought unfashionable than to reveal her personal horror. That she had been born with two teeth, Evangelina thought with some disappointment, wasn't a horror, just an anomaly. Her baby teeth had been exactly where they were supposed to be, they'd just developed before she was born.

What, though, of vagina teeth? Russell liked to talk about vagina teeth, the toothed vagina, vagina dentata, and was so enamored of the idea that he had once insisted Evangelina watch *Teeth* with him, calling it a horror movie, a cult classic, precisely the sort of movie she would typically avoid. When Evangelina thought of the movie now it seemed more comedy than horror, and she had found much delight in the movie though she did not share this with Russell. Evangelina had not been able to fully sort out her feelings about the movie, but she did know she liked Dawn, the chaste teenager afflicted with vagina teeth that chomped off men's penises and fingers when she did not want them inside of her. "No! I said stop!" Dawn had screamed as Tobey raped her, and when Tobey's face turned white and screaming, Evangelina felt relieved, even delighted as the severed penis thudded softly to the floor of the cave. She wanted to laugh, but Russell was wincing beside her, legs squeezed together, hands protectively covering his groin, so Evangelina did not laugh, but she did smile.

Terrible as vagina dentata might seem, Evangelina felt empathy with Dawn, and she did not feel bad for any of the men who had gotten exactly what they deserved, nor did she feel bad for Russell. His reaction gave her a thrill she could not admit to him or fully explore for herself, but she liked watching him squirm. He'd chosen the film, after all, so let him suffer the consequences. But what would it be like to have vagina teeth, Evangelina wondered. What would it be like to have teeth inside her vagina where no one would expect them, teeth that defended her, protected her, that backed up her choices about her own body?

Vagina dentata, despite its Latin-sounding name, was not real. Evangelina knew vagina teeth were an urban legend, a folktale at best, and this disappointed her. What was real was the story of Ashik Gavai in Mumbai, India, who had had 232 teeth removed from his jaw, who surely took no joy in his difference but was only glad those tragic miraculous teeth were now gone.

Evangelina Stays at the Hotel Blake

Chicago, Russell had said, would be a getaway. Just the two of them downtown for their twenty-second anniversary. Evangelina knew she'd brought this on herself. Every so often she just had to mention the trips her friend Tobi Ann had been on. Tobi Ann's husband Earl liked to travel, and they had been so many places—Cancun, Hawaii, New York City, even Alaska where Tobi Ann had seen the Northern Lights. What Evangelina wouldn't give to see the Northern Lights! Every year Tobi Ann and Earl would, without fail, take yet another anniversary trip like they had never grown out of being in love. It made Evangelina feel a little sick inside to see the way Tobi Ann and Earl carried on out in public, not so much the hand holding—even Russell did that from time to time, and Evangelina didn't mind as she liked when people smiled at them—but the way Earl would slip up behind Tobi Ann and slap her bottom, playful-like. Russell used to do that with her, Evangelina thought, back when they were newlyweds, but she couldn't recall whether she'd ever really liked it, and even if she once had, she knew she no longer did. These days it made Evangelina nervous when Russell so much as hugged her at the end of a long day, and she braced herself in case he wanted more than just a hug.

But now they were in Chicago, having traveled the South Shore Line from South Bend that morning, and Russell had checked them into the Hotel Blake because, for Chicago, the Hotel Blake was reasonably priced at $150 a night through Expedia, plus it was not too far from places to go and things to see that might keep Evangelina busy. Chicago wasn't as exotic as Cancun or Hawaii, New York City or Alaska, but it was bigger than Elkhart and some distance away, and while Chicago wouldn't exactly impress Tobi Ann, Chicago was better than nothing at all. Maybe she could even get some new shoes on clearance at Marshall Fields that would be better than the Kohl's clearance shoes she usually wore.

Evangelina had to admit, not to Russell but quietly in her mind, that she really was quite taken with both the Hotel Blake and the sturdy bellhop with the cropped gray hair who bowed and said "At your service, m'lady," when she entered. Like in Downton Abbey days, Evangelina thought, cementing her assessment that this truly could have been a hotel worthy of Lord and Lady Grantham, especially as the plaque outside proclaimed the Hotel Blake to be on the National Register of Historic Places. Evangelina liked both the history of the place and how the bellhop had attended to her, which had made her feel seen somehow.

"What a stunning couple!" the bellhop said, looking, Evangelina was sure, at her and not at Russell still catching his breath from walking the luggage six blocks from the train station. "Stunning couple," the bellhop had said, and Evangelina liked the sound of that, though more the "stunning" than the "couple" if she were being honest.

Riding on the elevator to their room, Evangelina stood slightly behind and to the side of the bellhop, which meant she had no choice but to breathe in the bellhop's scent of sweat and a spicy musk cologne. She couldn't quite tell where the cologne began and the sweat stopped, she only knew she liked-and-didn't-like it in the way she liked-and-didn't-like the tang of taco meat, which made her feel suddenly hungry though she'd eaten a meal's worth of snacks on the train.

"What brings you to the Windy City?" the bellhop asked in a voice Evangelina liked for its combined strength and softness. Tongue-tied, Evangelina looked down and saw the bellhop's shiny black shoes with their perfectly even laces, shoes smaller than her own size nines and better kept. Evangelina thought of her own stubby toes and wondered about the bellhop's, which she imagined to be long and slender and warm inside the thick black socks, toes she imagined to be like Rose's had been. "Anniversary," Russell grunted without much enthusiasm, Evangelina thought, and this bothered her because even though she realized herself to be indifferent about the anniversary getaway, in moments like this in an elevator heading to the 7th floor of the Hotel Blake in downtown Chicago, she wanted her reason for being in the city to matter deeply to her, and to people like this friendly bellhop, so she shied away from the bellhop, took her husband's hand in hers, leaned into his side and said, "Twenty-two years." She gave Russell a little squeeze. The bellhop smiled a smile Evangelina thought looked forced. "Twenty-two years? Wow! You don't hear that much these days."

"We know," Evangelina said giving Russell a kiss on the cheek, but Russell said nothing and she herself felt stiff and uncertain. "Well," said the bellhop, "Stick around until Wednesday and you can do Taste of Chicago." But today was just Monday, and Russell had only gotten the deal on the room for one night, and, really, that was enough time to celebrate their twenty-two years together, but all the same, the bellhop was thoughtful to have mentioned it.

All Evangelina really wanted for her anniversary was a room with a view. Certainly, she knew that Chicago was not an E. M. Forster novel, nor was it a 1980s movie starring Helena Bonham-Carter based on an E. M. Forster novel, but the things that mattered a hundred years ago still mattered now. She was certain of that. If Evangelina was to be in the Windy City for her twenty-second anniversary, she wanted a room from where she could see the Windy City, or at least some of it, given the reasonable price Russell had paid for their room and the concessions that must therefore be made. Evangelina longed to see towering skyscrapers with all their beautiful windows and architecture of an earlier time, so sturdy, stone, and vertical, so symmetrical and balanced. If she were not to be on a beach somewhere in the Caribbean like Tobi Ann so often was, then at least she wanted the very best view she could possibly have in Chicago.

So it was that when the bellhop showed Russell and her into room 717, while Russell could not for the life of him manage to find any dollar bills in his wallet to tip the bellhop, Evangelina looked straight ahead to the window at the end of the room and through it saw the side of a white brick building. That was no view. Evangelina composed herself while Russell fumbled in his pockets and handed over his assorted change, and when the bellhop said, "I guess I'll leave you to it" and winked at her, Evangelina was certain, Evangelina laughed too high and too loud because if she didn't, she would despair. That, she thought again, turning to the window, was no view. No view at all. They might as well have stayed in Elkhart and done nothing for all the good it was to come to Chicago to stay at the Hotel Blake and have no view at all.

Evangelina flung her purse down onto the bed closest to the window—she always liked Russell to book rooms with two double beds—then threw herself down on the bed. The white comforter felt smooth and cool against her cheek, luxurious even. She ran her hands across the comforter, but this sudden bodily comfort was not enough. It just wasn't. She thought of Tobi Ann. This never would have happened to Tobi Ann. Earl would have gotten Tobi Ann a room with a view. And not only would Earl not have gotten a room with any old view, Earl would have gotten a room in The Blackstone where she could have looked out at the beauty and wonder of Lake Michigan instead of this dratted white wall. Not that she begrudged Russell the hotel he had chosen at the price he had found—how could she when it was she who had insisted he find something reasonable?

Evangelina heard Russell settle himself onto the other bed and started to get up to tell him exactly what she thought. Then she saw it. At a slant, a view of tall buildings of various styles, skyscrapers even, against a bright blue summer sky. Perhaps, Evangelina thought, this might be okay after all. The rooftop of a parking garage was lackluster, to be sure, but the rest to her seemed spectacular—a brick building like Jimmy Stewart's in *Rear Window*, and a skyscraper with a statue of an angel (or was it a mermaid?) on top. Evangelina's view was attractively stacked and arranged and had a certain symmetry that made everything feel right with Chicago and right within her. These buildings had depth and squared corners and windows—lots of windows—for people to look out of and for her to look into.

And then, just to the right of the angel . . . what was it . . . a tan-colored flat panel pressing up against the sky. Strange. A building with no depth. Why, she couldn't see more than the building's front, not even a corner. Magnificent and rising up tall like the skyscraper it was! But windows. Where were its windows? She narrowed her eyes and saw little slits, hardly windows at all, like cracks that let the light in. Evangelina stood alongside her own window, traced the building upwards with her eyes, then down again, taking it all in as it took her breath away.

Then Russell came up alongside her and leaned over to look, placed his hand on Evangelina's shoulder and said, "Well, would you look at that?" He pointed up, up all the way to the top and Evangelina could see then that this was something like in one of Russell's science fiction movies with an opening way up on top, where men dressed in orange and white stood. Odd. How peculiar for men to be wearing orange and white on a rooftop in downtown Chicago. It gave her pause.

"Damn," Russell said, "That must be like the city jail or something."

Evangelina froze. She'd been looking straight at a prison and didn't recognize it for what it was. She looked up again and the men at the top were clearly looking down, watching something, watching somebody. Watching . . . her? What a view they must have had with no white wall to block them!

Two of the men pressed against the fence, arms arced above their heads, stretched high with fingers curled around the wire. She knew what that felt like to look through wire fence. She had done it as a child at the perimeter of her elementary school playground, fingers curled around wire, eyes peering through the little holes to the street outside and the people walking by, so it was as if she weren't even behind a fence, her vision taking in the whole of the world, her body inside a cage but her eyes free to look as long and as far as she wanted. She never much liked school, well, not so much school she didn't like but recess, wondering what she was supposed to do with other kids or even by herself and never quite figuring it out, though she tried, sometimes, to play with the other girls but mostly she just stood back and watched, or stood close enough to be able to listen and nod but never really to get a word in edgewise, so she was always glad to leave the playground and return to the classroom where she knew what to do. Sometimes she felt like that with Russell, not exactly knowing what to do and say when they had empty time. Maybe that was why she always kept so busy.

Evangelina had forgotten the fence but now she remembered. Looking up at the prisoners in their rooftop exercise yard, she remembered how a wire fence felt cool on days like this, how she had always liked to curl her own fingers around the wire because of the pleasure the temperature and the texture gave. The metal had been rusty and rough but cool, and she would curl her fingers over the wire until she could no longer feel the coolness in her fingers, and then she would do that again and again as the fence warmed to her, sometimes until the end of recess. She was always relieved to return inside, but she also was glad to have had a fence to lean on through which she could watch everything beyond the playground. She wondered if having a wire fence could have helped her marriage or maybe just helped her, but how? She did not have words or understanding for what she felt and she scolded herself for feeling such a silly thing. Besides, she would have looked like a crazy woman, maybe even looked like a prisoner, if she spent her days peering out through a wire fence.

Crazy. Like those men in orange and white? But Russell didn't take note of the fence and the men looking out through it. What impressed Russell was that there was a prison in the middle of downtown Chicago. She could tell by the way he kept talking that the prison both impressed and baffled him, and when something baffled him, he kept working it over in his brain until he got it sorted. Of course, she also did this, but for Evangelina her ponderings were less directed, less about getting a definite answer than about imagining all the possibilities, and she never seemed capable of sorting anything at all. The prison looked flat like it had no depth, like it was nothing but a sheer panel rising into the sky. The flatness troubled Evangelina less than it troubled Russell for she had always been able to just accept and move on when she had a will to because, really, what was the point of questioning, especially when in questioning she might uncover truths she did not like? There had to be some sort of explanation, something she didn't know, but what she didn't know did not trouble her when it came to prisons in the middle of Chicago that occupied the central position in her view. She knew she was moderately troubled by the men inside being criminals, but not by the prison's architecture and not by the fence.

Russell, however, was bothered, and Evangelina could tell because he kept pacing back and forth in front of the window. Then he stopped, turned, pointed his finger toward the prison and whispered, "It's a goddamn triangle. That's why there are no corners." Evangelina felt in her body that small shock of disappointment that came now and then when Russell figured out something before her, but she quickly moved into a smile, a nod, and a "Yes, dear. It is a triangle. Bravo, Russell."

Evangelina knew she shouldn't be cruel, but while on some level it was comforting to have the explanation for why the building looked so flat, she knew Russell well enough to know that this wouldn't just be the end of his fascination, and for that she blamed his love of *The Shawshank Redemption.* "Now, how could a prisoner plan an escape?" he asked next, and the thought of a prison break while they were in Chicago on their twenty-second anniversary brought with it a thrill and a horror. She pictured in her mind Russell on the rooftop wearing an orange and white jumpsuit, engaging an old-timer who looked like Morgan Freeman in some crackpot escape plot. She knew in Russell's mind he was the Tim Robbins character, that he'd been imprisoned for a crime he hadn't committed, that he had to escape and get back home to her, the woman he loved. There was something noble in that, and she didn't mind being the center of his story in this way. She used to be, after all.

Twenty-two years ago she was the center of his story, and he was the center of hers. Now she was in Chicago with her husband and had nothing to say to him, and she didn't know why. When they talked, it was across each other and about different things. Russell talking *Game of Thrones* and prison breaks and how difficult the workers he oversaw at Martin's Super Market could be and the bills and sexy yoga, and, well, it just went on and on and on. What had they once talked about? What did they even have in common? She couldn't remember then, could only experience now, and that made imagining any future difficult.

Evangelina looked out from her window in the Hotel Blake and wondered at the narrow little slits of prison windows and what it would feel like to be a prisoner. She imagined herself in a small dark cell with metal bars on one side and the narrow window on the other. Stretched out on her prison cot, she would see light squeeze in over her, but to see outside, if she were able to see out at all, she was sure she would have to stand on her tiptoes and press her forehead up against indestructible glass. She thought of the bay window in her grandmother's home where as a child she had stretched out on Sunday mornings after church with a cold glass of orange juice and the Sunday comics, and Evangelina remembered the feeling of the warm sun, free for the taking, streaming through a window bigger than her, warming her whole self. Evangelina was almost certain that was not the experience of the men inside the prison. She had watched enough prison movies with Russell to know that. Why would you put slits of windows inside a prison? Tease the inmates with something they couldn't have? Why would you give them a little light when what they needed was a lot? And then she wondered, how much time did they get at the fence? An hour a day? An hour a week? Was it like a school recess? Just a few minutes to look at the view, feel the coolness of the fence?

"Good view, huh?" Russell said.

That fence between her fingers. She could almost feel it.

"I'm tired. I think I'll lie down," said Evangelina, closing the drapes.

Evangelina Has a Sudden Insight

In the entryway of her home, Evangelina hung her purse on the closet doorknob and set down her Marshall Fields bag containing her new pair of Italian leather shoes, deeply discounted and a half-size too small but she would wear them all the same. Evangelina was not exactly satisfied with how her anniversary getaway with Russell had gone, but she was also not entirely despondent, just a little on the tired side when she heard the familiar sound of cat claws scraping metal and looked to see Duchess standing on hind legs outside, her orange face visible through the glass. Evangelina thought to herself, "Maybe Russell loves me, and my mother says Jesus does too, but so does my cat meowing to be let in, and it is she that matters most."

Evangelina Feels a Tickle

Standing at the PetSmart check-out, Evangelina felt it, that newish tickle that happened now and then in the right front pocket of her jeans. It was a private sensation, this momentary tickle against her leg, something meant for her and only her. Evangelina hated ring tones at any volume, and the personalized tones people used to match callers' personalities were always so subjective, she thought, having more to do with the person who set the tone than the actual caller. Little judgments. That's what they were. Ring tones, even those that just sounded like a ringing telephone, were brash, obnoxious, and declamatory, and Evangelina did not need everybody knowing her business. Still, she did like the tickle. Oh, sure, Evangelina knew, most people called it a "buzz" and the phone manual called it "vibrate," but when she slipped her hand inside her pocket and her fingers glided over smooth glass, she felt that, yes, of all the possible words to use, "tickle" was the best of all.

She pulled out her new phone, a Moto G from Republic Wireless she had insisted on even though Russell said she didn't need to be that connected all the time and, in truth, to spite him because she, a grown woman, could make her own choices. Evangelina pressed the small black button on top, entered her passcode—POOREDITH—and checked her voicemail: a dental cleaning reminder. Nothing personal. Of course not. Not today when all her friends were either at work or on vacation. But they were on Facebook. So she touched the little blue square with the friendly white "f" and another world opened up to her. A little red square at the top with the number "1" inside popped up against the backdrop of the globe, a symbol of the world, of universal connectedness.

Evangelina was hopeful. She would readily admit that she was new to this smartphone world and newer still to Facebook, but she had 36 friends now and they were always posting things of interest. Well, of interest to them, Evangelina thought, but not always of interest to her. Still, she was hopeful that this post would be of interest, so she lifted her finger and brought it up to the small red square and rested it there, just for a second, until Lisa Nicely's post revealed itself: "I ask for American on my burger and Steak 'n Shake gives me Swiss? WTF? Morons!"

Evangelina sighed, slid the phone back into her pocket, and watched as the man with the cart full of cans of Friskies salmon pâté moved forward and placed just one can on the counter. This man, Evangelina thought, was a good customer. She felt a slight thrill that she was waiting behind a man with one hundred or more items in his cart but all the same bar code, which could be scanned once and multiplied by the cashier. Simple. Clean. Efficient. She studied the man's navy-blue pea coat covered with cat fur of all colors and wondered how many cats he had, whether he lived alone with all of them. Evangelina knew that if she were ever to have more than her Duchess, Russell would have none of it, would have none of her. Evangelina would have to move out, live alone, buy cases of Friskies to feed all the cats she would surely accumulate in her … despair? In her freedom?

Evangelina didn't know how a life with cats but not a husband would be, but in that moment, she wondered if it might be better. She watched the man remove crumpled bills from his wallet with his ruddy and wrinkled right hand, along the back of which was a raw red scratch, fresh and puffy. His hand trembled as he handed the bills to the cashier, and his age worried Evangelina. What if he died alone? What if his cats ate him? Evangelina shut out the thought, determined he was a fool and not somebody she could ever become. She had given her heart to Duchess and would give her heart to no more, and she would let the stability of her marriage be enough. After twenty-two years together, Russell wasn't going anywhere and neither would she. No.

Again, the tickle. Or was it? She wasn't sure, but she pulled her phone from her pocket just in case, lit up the screen, entered POOREDITH and saw there were no new notifications. But surely something had happened in the space of time since she had last looked, so she opened Facebook and scrolled through pictures of kittens, a meme about Obamacare, the thoughts and happenings of her non-preferred friends. Then the cashier's voice broke through. "Ma'am, I need you to put away your phone and place your items on the counter." Evangelina's face flushed. She had never wanted to be one of those rude phone users who held up lines and didn't talk to people around them, didn't notice anything but their glowing little screens, but here she was having crossed over, having become a person she despised. She put her phone in her pocket and placed on the counter a bag of Iams Proactive Health Sensitive Digestion and Skin, a ten-pack of catnip mice, and a new blue cat bed Duchess didn't need but at 60% off she couldn't pass it up even if

Russell didn't approve. He'd just have to get over it like he had gotten over the 52-inch faux fur cat tree and condo she'd bought last month. Evangelina knew the etiquette of not answering her phone or looking at messages, but still she had, and now she had been shamed, but what could she say, really, to the cashier? Nothing.

Sometimes Evangelina felt like the woman in that Old Testament story. She didn't know the woman's name, never seemed able to remember it, and why should she? Maybe the woman didn't even have a name, or, rather, hadn't been given one in the story, for everybody had a name, right? Even a concubine. But how could a name even be remembered against such horrors? What was it that had happened to her? Had she been raped? Her body defiled? Raped until she died, yes. That was it, wasn't it? And then she had been made a warning to others, hadn't she? That much Evangelina felt certain she remembered. Cut up into how many parts—legs, arms, hands, feet, toes, kneecaps, elbows, everything, cut off and scattered to how many places? Twelve? She thought for sure it was twelve. One for each tribe.

Evangelina wondered what had happened to the woman's heart. The story hadn't said. Sent someplace far away, she was sure, never to reunite with all the other parts of her. That's how Evangelina felt. Scattered. Like she was far flung in all directions with only her mind still here to remember, sort of remember, having ever been whole. Evangelina never knew what to make of these feelings when they came upon her. It was like knowing she had once been . . . no . . . wondering whether she ever had been whole and connected and useful in some way. Oh, certainly, in many ways it was better this way, better not to feel everything all at once as a creature, a creature like the red-tailed hawk she had seen sitting on the top of the telephone pole at the edge of the highway one frozen February morning at sunrise. She had seen it from a distance, so still, like a statue, but so focused, so concentrated, like a ball of energy had been made solid and taken form in this hawk that watched and waited, that just was. She knew when it moved, when it finally flew, it would be with purpose, with intent to kill, but wasn't that the way of the wild? It wasn't the way of her life. And she sometimes wished it were.

Evangelina Dreams of a Train

Evangelina fell asleep in her La-Z-Boy, her phone still aglow with the BBC headline, "Trump Retweets Quote Attributed to Fascist Leader Mussolini," and then she dreamed. Dreamed of a train going somewhere and she on it, thinking maybe at the end there was a vacation destination and that she had won this trip, only there were so many on this train and standing room only and she was walking toward where she believed the bathrooms were, only there were no bathrooms, just a little dip in the flooring so the muck wouldn't run upwards and she was advised to slide her shoes back on before getting that far and this, this was her first real sign that maybe there was not after all a vacation destination awaiting her at the end of this line, which was when everything shifted and Evangelina found herself outside at a train station watching a stopped train as it began to pull out of the station, and in her hands she held red potatoes with words carved into them, words that were poems, poems that were potatoes, and so she hustled up to the front of the train, handing out potatoes to passengers who reached out their hands, feeling she wasn't doing enough but she was doing something and that maybe these potatoes, these poems, would fill a hunger in some.

Evangelina Waits by the Side
of the Road

She had no choice but to stand by the road and wait. That was just what one did when a car broke down, Evangelina knew. Wait for somebody to come along who could help. Evangelina didn't like waiting. She had been in a hurry to drive out to see her nephew Nick in Angola, Nick who also had gotten stuck on the side of the road the day before but stuck in a different way, not with a flat tire like hers but with a totaled car, his mother's—her sister Lucille's—navy blue Buick LeSabre. Evangelina recognized the difference between her experience and Nick's, of course. For her, the "check tires" dashboard indicator light had lit up and she had pulled off the main road and onto 300 West, one of those country roads so insignificant it was numbered, not named. She got out and walked around the car, seeing the problem in the passenger front tire which wasn't as firm as the others, which sank down low to the ground. Evangelina had been in a hurry to get somewhere, and the flat tire was inconvenient, nothing more.

That Nick's body had been thrown free of the twisted metal and shattered windshield was harder for Evangelina to imagine than had he been trapped inside, a prisoner with the doors and windows closed around him, requiring rescue workers to use the jaws of life she had seen so often on the

WNDU nightly news to save him. Not that Nick could have walked away anyway had he just been trapped. Wrecks like that you couldn't walk away from and Nick with his back and three ribs broken, left lung punctured, skull split, and skin abrased, hadn't walked away but instead blacked out until an ambulance arrived and EMS workers scooped him up from the edge of the road like so much roadkill. Evangelina didn't like to think about being stranded in that way, the way Nick had been. His accident seemed so unfair, so wrong, and so she had been talking endlessly about it with strangers so she didn't have to think about it, did not have to come to terms with it.

Evangelina leaned up against her car prepared to wave down any car, truck, or even bicycle that might pass. She didn't know for how long she stood, only that it was long enough for her feet to feel tired and for her lower back to begin to ache. But in all this time, however long it actually was, nobody, not so much as a tractor, came down the road. So she walked around to the passenger side where she could sit in the grass and spindly buckhorn growing at the edge of the ditch.

She had messed up with her new cellphone. Evangelina knew that. Russell had trained her (and that was the word Russell had used, "trained") to take the phone on the road but some days like today she forgot to bring the car charger and her phone had given out some time ago while trying unsuccessfully to use the navigation feature to get to where she meant to go without having to unfold a paper map, which would have been easier, but people weren't doing that these days, Russell had said. Evangelina's phone was a low-end model and so only moderately smart, and her signal wasn't much good out in the northeast Indiana countryside.

"GPS signal has been lost," said the voice on her phone ten miles out, and as she fumbled to type in the coordinates while she steered down a road with too many turns, her phone emitted its familiar bright tones of goodbye and shut down.

And then the tire had gone flat.

Evangelina had a spare in her trunk. Russell always made sure of that. But Evangelina did not know how to even begin to remove the flat tire and put on the spare, not because she hadn't tried to pay attention all those many times her father and later Russell had told and shown her, but because despite the demonstrations and practice, she didn't know how, and besides, it was the sort of thing she might start successfully but then mess up entirely. So Evangelina sat on the edge of the road, thinking that anybody who happened along would see her and ask if she needed help. Surely, that was how things were done in the country. They were friendly out in the country, after all, except for the occasional scary man in a falling down family farmhouse, but she hadn't seen any such houses on her drive, and besides, such men were not inclined to leave theirs.

But what caught Evangelina's attention most weren't her own thoughts about the strangers who might happen by to help her—a mother toting children back and forth to Vacation Bible School perhaps, or an older gentleman who knew how to change a tire but could do so without Russell's comments about her lack of ability. A mother would have given her a ride into town, and the older gentleman would have changed the tire himself. Either way, it would have been a win and some help for her, with none of the self-consciousness or shame to go along with her lack of knowledge and ability. And in a way, letting somebody else help her, that would make them feel good too.

Still, that wasn't what Evangelina was thinking about just now as she sat by the ditch and gazed out across a gently rolling field covered with green soybeans, bright and perky and drinking up the water from last night's rain. Refreshed, Evangelina thought. That must have been how the little plants felt. The thought made Evangelina thirsty but not so thirsty as to return to the car for a bottle of water and a Crystal Light lemonade packet she kept for times like these, which, fortunately, weren't many, though she was beginning to think this one, this being stuck on a country road with a flat tire and no phone to call anybody wasn't so very bad, and it surprised her to think it as even Russell who never noticed anything about her liked to say how busy she was all the time.

Evangelina stretched her legs and leaned forward so her hands touched her bare knees then rubbed down to her calves before straightening and looking again out to the field. Evangelina found she did not want to move, and it was strange, Evangelina thought, sitting where she was doing nothing. She wasn't hot or the least bit irritated and realizing this surprised her because even Evangelina knew herself to be the sort of person inclined to be hot and irritated. Quite the reverse, actually. Evangelina felt almost pleasant the way she had over six years ago when she had practiced yoga, and she felt again how good it was to clear her mind and breathe deep and long.

When Evangelina began her morning drive, the announcer on Cool Hits Radio had said that the weather would be cloudy and cool with the sun only emerging later in the day. Evangelina had been glad about that, having always greeted summer with a kind of dread, and though she never could explain why she had felt this way, she knew it to be how she was. Maybe it had to do with everybody moving around wearing fewer clothes, Evangelina thought, how she never knew what part of a person's body she was supposed to look at, where to put her eyes, and how embarrassed that made her feel. For that reason, though Evangelina had memories of loving to swim with her cousin Jo, she told herself she had no desire to let the sun bake her skin brown, and that that was normal enough for a woman her age. She preferred just enough of a chill to inhibit sweat and justify full body coverings and so dreaded summer with its heat and sunshine intensity drawing water from the ground and energy from her, leaving her feeling depleted.

But right now wasn't like that for Evangelina, even knowing as she did that the heat would certainly come. She touched the grass to her sides. The blades felt cool and swollen. She plucked a blade and broke it open, touched her finger to the edge and felt just a hint of wetness. This was how she imagined the soybeans in the field before her to be, all growing and holding onto their moisture, letting themselves be a bit greener and more luscious in the dampened soil, which hadn't yet felt enough heat to crack and still held onto its fertility.

Evangelina looked before her and imagined she could walk forever in that field because it was just that beautiful. Evangelina looked back at her shiny Oldsmobile she had just that morning run through the five-dollar car wash down the road from her house, then turned back to the field. The car was fine, Evangelina knew, just a flat tire caused by a slow leak. No drama beyond the small flashing of a dashboard light saying, "check tires." Evangelina was glad the leak had been slow, that she hadn't blown a tire, that her tire could, whenever help arrived, be replaced by the spare, which even now waited in her trunk for somebody to come along who had the confidence to do such things.

Evangelina breathed in. The car was fine.

Evangelina breathed out. She was fine too.

Evangelina stretched her arms up to the sun in salutation. She would live.

Evangelina would live and Nick might not, and this thought worried her but also made her appreciate that even now, in this moment, they both were still alive in the world. How remarkable! Other days a flat tire would have rattled her, would have worried and concerned and stressed her beyond measure. Evangelina knew that about herself. Today, though, was different.

Evangelina heard an approaching car but couldn't bring herself to stand and wave it down and thought this had to do with the beans in the field, how beautiful they were, so she stood and walked toward them, lifting her legs high to step over a barbed wire fence. Walking into the field, the clouds shifted and the sun cast down, illuminating the soft leaves of soy beans. From where Evangelina had been sitting, she hadn't seen the sparkles of water, but she saw them now, hundreds on one tiny leaf, and crouched to touch the leaf, knowing the dew would be gone soon enough, evaporated by the sun. She stood again and looked out, feeling on her shoulder the sun's sudden unrelenting warmth. The heat felt good, felt just right. Had the leaves not been waving in front of her, she would not even have known there was a breeze. The world felt so still.

Evangelina Listens to Music

Evangelina didn't know why she stood in Martin's Super Market aisle four before columns and rows of saltines laid out before her in a predictable grid, listening. She didn't know why she kept listening to music without any words, but as she stood there she remembered singing "I'd Like to Teach the World to Sing (In Perfect Harmony)" with her mom and all the smiling people on the mountaintop on TV holding their bottles of Coke. So unlike her to listen, she knew, even as she couldn't move, couldn't just pull herself away, choose her saltines, and get on with checking off the items on her two-page list. Still, she stood, having been stopped by a twinge in her chest that was growing into an ache, a swell, a wave that might just drown her in the middle of Martin's. She knew all this, and still, Evangelina stood.

Evangelina hated the inconvenience of sudden tears when Kleenex was the last item at the bottom of her list and four aisles down in aisle eight, so far away from where she stood willing herself to stare through her tears as if they weren't even there. There was no reason for this, Evangelina told herself, putting her hands over her ears and willing her brain to regain control, to keep herself in check. *Stop it, Evangelina,* she scolded herself. *Just stop it*. But she couldn't. And this frustrated her because most times she could.

Evangelina had long dismissed music as an inconvenience, an interrupter, and here it was grinding her gears to a halt, Evangelina realized, staring at Nabiscos, Spartans, and Zestas in their four uniform varieties of unsalted tops, salted tops, whole wheat, and reduced sodium varieties without taking in any of it, so full she was of sound.

And she didn't know why.

Evangelina, certain of how she looked to the mother pushing her cart through the aisle in smooth broad curves for the amusement of her laughing daughter, reached meaningfully for the Zesta Originals, turned the box over to examine the nutrition facts. She knew she looked like an oddity, a sad and useless thing made all the more absurd by her reading nutrition facts of a product made of so few bland ingredients—flour, oil, salt, and a handful of enrichments. Bland. Evangelina was overcome by the blandness of saltines and the blandness of her. She felt naked and pasty white, exposed to the eyes of the world, or at least the 10 a.m. Wednesday morning shoppers, even as the echoes of mother-daughter love subsided. Evangelina felt inside a deep trembling as her tears turned from trickles to torrents, some dam inside her burst at last.

Stop it, Evangelina. Just stop it, she screamed inside her own head. *How old are you anyway? Shape up! Get a hold on yourself.* Evangelina gripped the Zesta box so hard she dented the side crease. *Goddammit! Now look what you've done.* The voice in her head was her own, but still it shocked her. Unsteady now, she put the Zestas back on top of the column. Looking at them straight on from the end, the red Zesta box looked perfect, untouched, in line with all the rest. But Evangelina knew about the damage, even if nobody else would notice, even if nobody else would have cared.

Evangelina wished the wordless song would end. Evangelina wished the song would go on forever. Evangelina wished to stay in the moment and to escape from it and to just dissolve into the floor or fly away like the sparrows she sometimes saw trapped and flitting around the supermarket ceiling, not quite free but also not wholly bound. Evangelina wished . . . she didn't know what she wished . . . just felt this bubbly synthesized knock-off churning up something inside too big, too grand, too frightening.

Evangelina stared at the saltine grid until the columns and rows of colors blurred into a cracker-y mosaic.

There aren't even any words. So how . . . ?

Once upon a time Evangelina listened on purpose, listened with her whole self, listened to records she alone had chosen on her small suitcase record player, a gift from her mother for her thirteenth birthday. How was it, she wondered now as she felt a surge of loss, that she had once listened to whatever moved her in the moment? How was it that she had once given herself permission to listen to whatever she desired? How was it she had had no rules for herself then, no lists to follow? How was it she had stretched out across the quilt her grandmother had made from fabric that Evangelina had helped her choose and cut into perfect squares, her eyes just taking it all in, letting herself be taken away to somewhere else, even as she let herself be right where she was with melodies and sung poetry wrapping themselves around her.

She smelled the cedar of the keepsake box she always kept open, the one she had purchased at Rock City with the two dollars her father had given her to spend the summer she turned eight. She felt the soft weight of Smokey walking across her body, turning once, twice, then curling round and lying down upon her chest, a weight and a rhythm of purr poured into her. She heard "The Sound of Silence" on her record player, and felt the silence as though it were a heavy blanket, its only purpose to calm her. But how could she be calm? Evangelina had been caught off guard by a wordless tune in Martin's on a busy Wednesday with things to do, items to cross off, expectations to be met that Russell, no, not even Russell, that she had laid out for herself.

She changed the record in her mind to *Circles in the Stream,* a live album her grandfather had passed down on condition that she pronounce the musician's name correctly. "The Canadian way," he had said, "Bruce *Co-burn*," then had her repeat it twice. Don't say it like it's spelled," he had said, shaking his finger. "If I catch you saying '*Cock-burn*', I'll take the record back." Then he had winked and smiled— in memory, her grandfather was always smiling—and Evangelina set the imagined needle down in the opening groove of "God, Bless the Children." She watched the record spin as she listened for that line about pain, remembering how it had sounded so poetic when she was a teenager, but feeling now the truth of it. She felt run over by a steamroller and wondered if what her grandfather's favorite Canadian had sung explained what had happened to her. Had she let it happen? Made it happen? She didn't know the cause, could only feel the effect, but if she let herself feel the full hurt of loss, she wouldn't make it through her list.

Evangelina missed then her grandmother's quilt, missed running her fingers along the stitching at the squares' edges, missed studying with her eyes and fingertips the purposefulness and precision of squares in tandem with the randomness of colors, designs, textures. Stripes to solids to dots to flowers. Blues to oranges to blacks to pinks. Smooth satin to soft cotton to rough denim. Each square its own world, and hundreds of worlds stitched together with threads of love, memory, heartache, longing. Evangelina closed her eyes, breathed deeply, and smelled unmistakably her grandmother in all the particularities of smell—Rose Milk lotion, potatoes and onions fried up in bacon grease, moth balls, Juicy Fruit gum, Murphy's Oil Soap, and a hint of old lady.

Evangelina missed her grandmother's voice so she conjured it up for herself—so effortless, so immediate, so present she couldn't have said whether it was her mind doing the work or whether her grandmother really was there with her.

Evie, honey, come in here, won't you, and give your grandma a hand with these tomatoes. Grandpa will be in from the garden any minute and he'll be hungry, so let's get supper on the table for him.

Evie, honey, you go on over there and play me a piano roll, won't you? Something nice. How about "It Only Happens When I Dance With You"? I'll finish up the dishes and you get those feet to pumping pedals.

You're my girl, Evie, honey. You know that don't you, Evie girl? I always wanted an Evie for a granddaughter, and here you are standing in this kitchen with me. Isn't that something?

Evangelina's knees buckled. She grabbed the cart to keep from falling to the floor even as she collapsed inside. Her grandmother never would have taken to calling her Evangelina, she knew, and she was filled with sudden longing to be her grandma's Evie—Evie honey, Evie child, just Evie—once more. Had it been such a bad name? She had loved her name most when her grandmother had said it, had loved herself most then too. But her grandmother was gone now, had been for twenty-six years, and Evangelina fit who she was now like a stiff, certain, confining, self-correcting glove. Those times the glove had come close to being pulled off, she had just pulled it on all the tighter.

You never have to be anything but Evie, she heard her grandmother sing in tune to the song over the Martin's loudspeaker. *You never have to be anything but you, Evie honey.* As her grandmother's voice faded, music filled the void, returned her to her quilt, her bed where she rolled over on her stomach and propped herself up on her elbows, calmed by the delicate silver arm bobbing up and down ever so gently with the motion of the record turning round, as if it were a gull riding endlessly on an ocean current. Every word she'd ever heard on every one of those records, every note passed through her, the songs so deep inside she knew them all by heart even now when she no longer listened, no longer let herself listen. She had been Evie then, she remembered. Evie who loved music, who lived her life in the pauses between the notes.

Evangelina did not, could not, admit to herself that that was why she no longer listened, but she knew. To go there again? To let notes, chords, rhythms, lyrics get inside where they could change everything? With Rose, music had almost destroyed Evangelina, almost saved her too. Every day, Rose had sent her a new song, and Evangelina had added each song to a YouTube playlist she'd titled "Beautiful Things," the only playlist she had ever created.

Sometimes when Russell was at work, Evangelina sang "Guided By Wire" with Neko Case as she washed dishes and wiped down kitchen countertops.

Sometimes in the car, Evangelina listened to Ani DiFranco convict her with "If Yr Not."

Sometimes in bed on sleepless nights, Russell asleep beside her, Evangelina cried quietly as Passenger sang "Things That Stop You Dreaming" through her earbuds into her very soul.

Then Rose moved, and two weeks later Evangelina stopped listening, deleted the playlist, tried to forget, but how could she forget every word, note, and song? Evangelina never could, and in those rare moments with nothing to do when she allowed herself to think of Rose, she still sang every word of "Lucky" by Hem in her mind, and when nobody was around to hear, she sometimes even sang the words out loud.

Feeling was too hard, Evangelina told herself even as she knew she had been swallowed up by feeling. She had made her life so well-ordered with its purposeful lists of tasks to be completed, groceries to be bought, meals to be prepared and consumed, people to see and talk to but never let closer than arm's length. She couldn't bear to let music back inside, not even here in the saltine section of the cracker aisle. She had damaged the right-angled edges of a Zesta box and she knew, would always know, even if nobody could see the damage she had done.

Evangelina's tears had stopped, but she still stood staring at neatly ordered saltines, telling herself she hadn't really been crying. But she could feel the truth of her lie in the heat and sting of her face.

Over the grocery store speakers, "What the World Needs Now Is Love" played. Deep inside Evangelina the wordless songs had struck a single match, setting ablaze decades of dry kindling. This wasn't the sort of fire

Evangelina could use. This was a fire that would do as it wanted until it consumed everything and left her with . . . with what?

Evangelina crumpled her two-page list, left it behind in her half-filled cart, and rushed out of Martin's. The saltines would have to wait.

Evangelina Puts Out a Fire

It wasn't that Evangelina hadn't known of Autumn. She had. Autumn had lived next door for two years, or was it three? While looking out her kitchen window Evangelina often saw Autumn in her backyard, sometimes sitting in a rusted metal folding chair with an open sketchbook and charcoal pencils, sometimes standing with a paintbrush in her hand before a canvas that most times remained empty while Autumn drank one beer after another, but that sometimes would explode with vivid colors and unexpected shapes in ways that looked like nothing Evangelina had ever seen but belonged to a language of color and feeling she wanted to learn.

Autumn often half-danced, half-stumbled around her backyard, dropping her empty Coors cans on a wooden picnic table so weathered and gray that Evangelina could hardly tell it had once been painted red.

Evangelina watched. Always when Evangelina noticed Autumn, she just watched. And though Evangelina worried she shouldn't feel as she did, she found Autumn beautiful in the tender and sad way that she found falling autumn leaves beautiful in their moment between tree and ground, that moment that was not exactly freedom but more like unattachment when neither the tree nor the ground mattered but only the falling leaf in a brief embrace of air. Autumn in freefall, so beautiful, so lovely, so occupying her own skin when all Evangelina ever wanted was to split her aching skin and become something other than what she was.

And so Evangelina watched Autumn through her window.

Like Evangelina, Autumn had a husband, though a husband of a different sort than Russell who sometimes looked at Autumn but never saw her, Russell who looked at Autumn only long enough to call her "that drunk," Russell who shook his head at Autumn before wrapping his arms around Evangelina from behind to nuzzle her neck and say he was glad he had her and not Autumn for a wife, glad Evangelina was stable, reliable, known. How he and Evangelina had a good marriage compared to what Russell imagined it would be like to be married to crazy, drunk, artist Autumn, though he did think the sex must be good.

Evangelina would feel then the growth of something deep inside, something hard and round and smooth, something that in the beginning had been easy enough to ignore but had become less so with each accumulated layer over each accumulated year. She doubted Russell was right about any of what he said, but she couldn't put together the words to say otherwise, and why not let Russell believe what he wanted? It made him feel satisfied with how things were even if what Evangelina felt was something like sadness, even if a subtle snake hissed softly to her about her unhappiness. Why wasn't she happy? Why wasn't she happy when clearly Russell was being so loving toward her, wasn't he? He had his arms wrapped around her in the posture of marital bliss, or was it just marital security, or maybe marital entrapment? And why did she feel so lonely when Russell was around?

But that was Russell, not Jimmy, not Autumn's Jimmy who, when Evangelina thought of him thought also of Autumn's art, thought of that morning last spring she had been slicing strawberries at the sink for shortcake and seen Jimmy outside with Autumn when she was painting. Evangelina had watched Autumn spill herself out with colors on canvas and Jimmy, well Jimmy hadn't even once looked at Autumn's painting. Maybe that didn't mean Jimmy didn't like her art, but maybe he couldn't really see her art, and maybe not seeing her art meant he couldn't really see Autumn, like Autumn to him was no different than that nude silhouette Evangelina had seen on the mud flaps of so many sixteen wheelers, the silhouette that made her want to know who the woman was who had posed to be drawn that way in the first place.

Not that naked women bothered Evangelina. Evangelina wasn't prudish. But there was something about the unbeautiful and unremarkable and unspecific way of the silhouettes that troubled Evangelina, how they were all the same—featureless, dark, static—nothing like Autumn dancing in wide unsteady circles in the backyard with her tangled hair, thick and dark like a briar patch. Nothing like Autumn with her long thin fingers cradling a joint, something Evangelina had never smoked. Not like Autumn in her unbuttoned green flannel shirt, smoking as she watched the sun hatch in the sky, Evangelina feeling a burgeoning shiver of how beautiful Autumn was in all these ways and wondering whether Jimmy knew that about Autumn and wondering most if Autumn knew that about herself. No. Not like Autumn at all. Even when Autumn became her own drunken silhouette in the evening dark, she weaved through her yard like a fine dark thread. Autumn in Eveningland. That's how Evangelina thought of Autumn then, and Evangelina half-wondered what would happen if she were to tug that fine dark thread, wondered what would happen to Autumn and wondered even more what would happen to her, what such an unraveling might do to them both.

Of course, Evangelina told herself, she scarcely noticed Autumn. Not really. She just glanced at Autumn now and then while chopping onions or washing dishes or wiping down the kitchen counters after a Sunday morning breakfast, only half-wondered about the paintings she couldn't make full sense of but even more wondered about the charcoal sketches, especially the ones that so often went undrawn, the ones Evangelina believed were locked deep inside of Autumn in some private place that Evangelina hungered to know. Curiosity. Idle curiosity about her neighbor. That was all and there was nothing more to it, Evangelina told herself as she pulled closed the yellow-checkered curtains on the short valance. And why shouldn't Evangelina be curious? Everybody is curious about other people, aren't they? Everybody, right? That's why she'd majored in anthropology after all. Everybody, though maybe not so much Russell who was so quick and sure at assessing people: Autumn the drunk, Evangelina the secure wife. Well, maybe not everybody was curious in the way Evangelina was about other people, other people generally but most especially Autumn.

How was it that Evangelina felt certain that Autumn must also be curious about her? Or maybe it was just that Evangelina was curious about the possibility of Autumn being curious about her. Evangelina wondered what it was that she looked like through Autumn's eyes, Autumn's eyes rimmed with crow's feet that deepened when she smiled. What was it Autumn had seen in Evangelina those few times they'd been outside together in their separate yards, separated not by any fence or line that Evangelina could see but by something else, something harder to cross? What was it that Evangelina looked like, and did what Evangelina looked like to Autumn through Autumn's eyes have a name? She thought not, but still, she felt.

Had it been October? Had it been October when the fire had started? October when Autumn had decided to burn the pile of leaves she'd been raking on a day that had started warm and calm but by late afternoon had turned brisk and breezy? Had it been October or early November when Autumn had left behind her burning leaves to run to Evangelina's backyard and call, "Help me! Please help me!", words which Evangelina had to open her window to hear? Yes, October, Evangelina remembered, October right before Halloween, for there had been plain pumpkins on her back porch steps and carved jack-o-lanterns on Autumn's when they had rushed together through Evangelina's backyard and into Autumn's where they stood together witnessing the way the wind swooped up burning leaves from the pile in mini-flares, the way the wind sent the burning leaves spiraling up to the branches from which they had first fallen, burning themselves into ash before they could ignite the leaf cover below.

Autumn smelled boozy, Evangelina had thought as she walked with Autumn who leaned into her as if all that had separated them for so long was some tightly enforced idea in Evangelina's own mind of the distance between the two of them, the distance of affinity like Alice passing through the looking glass. Yes, this distance of affinity that for so long had kept her separate from this drunken artist who burned her leaves on breezy days. Evangelina felt the sharpness of Autumn against her side, against her shoulder, against her neck, and Evangelina didn't step away as she knew Russell would—Russell who always kept his distance from Autumn, always kept his distance from everybody, who was fond of calling Autumn . . . *oh, but not Russell . . . not Russell in my head again*, Evangelina pleaded with herself. *Not Russell, no no no, not Russell, not Russell right now.*

Autumn was in a state about the leaves and the fire and the wind and felt herself to blame for all of it, and when she, in all her turmoil, asked, "I'm not a drunk, Eve, am I? I'm not just a drunk, am I, Eve? Tell me I'm not," the words just hung there thick like smoke between them.

And then Evangelina said in one rushed and unstoppable exhale, "You are not a drunk, Autumn. You are beautiful." Evangelina knew that being an artist was who Autumn was and drinking, well, that was just something Autumn did, even if she did it a lot.

"I'm not a drunk, Eve," Autumn slurred. "Really, I'm a good person."

Eve. Something about being called Eve. About being called Eve by Autumn. Evangelina owned that. Evangelina had been called names, so many names—by others, by herself—but never Eve before, never a name that was the name of the first woman in the garden. But why would that name make her feel so bold? Evangelina remembered feeling this way before, remembered feeling this way with Rose.

Evangelina knew what to do with leaf fires, how to put them out, and this one, this pile of half-burning leaves, the rest being all smolder, was nothing really, hardly anything out of control, but it worried Autumn and so Evangelina grabbed from the side of Autumn's mustard-yellow metal shed the long-handled rake with the wide green plastic tines—six of them, one broken halfway up—and began spreading out the leaves from the fire that was less aflame than this woman who leaned even still into her, whose corduroy sleeve was wet with slopped beer, who smelled of cigarettes and weed, leaf smoke and sweat, whose head Evangelina could cradle perfectly between her shoulder and head, Evangelina liking the weight of Autumn's resting head and leaning body, liking the trust of Autumn's body against her own, liking that she was trusting her own body to be with Autumn's body, a reality unspoken and unthought, just felt.

"I'm going to be okay, aren't I, Eve?" Autumn asked, looking up at Evangelina who was gripped with a sudden knowing that she would give anything to swim deep in the hazel pools of Autumn's eyes. "Tell me I'm going to be okay. Please tell me I'm a good person, Eve." Those eyes and the spread of crow's feet in the weathered skin around them, and so Evangelina counted the furrows—one, two, three, four, five, six—six lines from where Autumn's eyelids met, six lines for the three toes on each foot of one ink-black crow, six lines that cupped the outer rim of Autumn's eye and Evangelina wishing she could touch those lines, could trace them, that's all, with her thumb and inside she felt . . . she felt . . . oh, she felt like she was drowning.

"I drink too much," Autumn said, her head dropping onto Evangelina's shoulder. "Eve, I drink too much, I know I do, but I'm still a good person. Tell me I'm going to be okay. Tell me we're going to be okay. We're going to be okay."

Evangelina lowered her head to rest against Autumn's, felt against her cheek the tangle of Autumn's soft hair that smelled of smoke and oranges. "Shh," Evangelina whispered, and then, "Hush now," and together they were quiet, quiet, and breathing softly. "You're a good person, Autumn,"

Evangelina said then. "You're a good person and you're going to be okay. We're both going to be okay. You're beautiful and you're going to be okay, we both are, both of us are going to be okay," which was when they both began to cry just a little, and so they sat down at the picnic table. Autumn took a beer from the half-emptied case and offered it to Evangelina who felt herself take the can in her hand, felt her finger pull back the tab, felt herself lift the beer to her dry lips and begin to drink this beer that was the temperature of the day and that tasted not bad and not good but tasted like a drink she was meant to drink even though Evangelina never drank more than a half-glass of Zinfandel, and only then at a holiday party so scared she was of losing control.

Evangelina had never been drunk in her whole life, never even been around anybody as drunk as Autumn was now. She had always left parties before the drinking really got going and felt awkward when she did drink because she knew nothing about alcohol although sometimes she wanted to even if most times she didn't care but sometimes did because drinking—really drinking—was a rite of passage she'd never let herself have, and here she was now, forty-four and clueless about what it meant to sit on a picnic bench in a backyard with a beautiful drunk artist whose leaves had caught fire on a breezy October day. Evangelina didn't know whether to leave or stay but stayed because Autumn had given her this beer, which she might as well drink and then maybe drink another and another after that. She felt both out of place and right where she belonged close to Autumn as this new Eve Autumn had called out of her, this Eve that had been spoken from Autumn's soft smiling mouth and so had come to be, this Eve who made Evangelina shiver through the snaking smoke, which rose from Autumn's still-smoldering leaves.

Evangelina Spoons with Russell

And so it was that in the weeks and months after Evangelina had extinguished Autumn's burning leaves, Evangelina still felt—still let herself feel—the full-body shiver of that October moment, that moment that had been only a moment, not a day, not even so long as to be called an afternoon. Each time she felt that moment she felt an increasing intensity as though she were again experiencing it for the first time squared by memory and distance so that inside she trembled, even if outwardly the most she could imagine that Russell could ever have said about her was that Evangelina seemed "distant," though in truth Russell hardly thought about Evangelina at all.

That's how it was on nights when Evangelina felt Russell spoon his body around hers, felt him wrap his arms around her in what she knew he would call embrace but to her felt like entrapment, though she wished that were not the word to come to mind. Evangelina felt her husband's breath hot against the side of her face even as her heart, her woefully and wonderfully wandering heart as she had grown to think of it, traveled back to that moment when Autumn—drunk, so drunk—had wrapped herself around Evangelina, that moment when Evangelina had let herself become this Eve that Autumn had called out of her who could and did wrap her arms around Autumn in response.

And though it was only Autumn who had spoken, only Autumn who had slurred, "I love you. I don't know why I love you, but I do," Evangelina had felt something like a shiver that had become a flash that had ignited her parched and desert heart, which still smoldered all these months later even on into February, the month set aside for romantic love. Only with Russell love wasn't like that, and she didn't know if it could ever be again, if it ever had been in the first place, which she felt more and more certain it hadn't. Evangelina couldn't begin to untwist the pretzel that she had contorted herself into with Russell, only knew what she had felt with Autumn in the moment of the leaves and knew what she had felt standing in Rose's driveway all those years ago. What had she felt and what did she continue to feel in her body first with Rose and now with Autumn? She didn't know whether the word "romantic" applied to either of those moments when romantic was a word she had never understood, only knew she had felt the word "love" in a way that didn't need to be defined.

Even now as Evangelina felt herself gripped so tightly by Russell, she remembered how she had not let go of Autumn, how, feeling secure, she had just held on as Autumn was holding onto her, confused but compelled and all wrapped up in the smell of leaves and fire and smoke and cheap beer and sweat that was Autumn, feeling something that she did not need to call anything—love or romance or lust or sin or anything at all—but that she could just let happen, just let be as it was because she was held—that's all, just held—in a way that Russell couldn't hold her. Held in a way that held space for Evangelina to hold and be held even as she knew that it wasn't Autumn she needed but something inside herself that Autumn had exposed when she cracked her open, some honesty in Evangelina's body that either she'd forgotten or that she'd never known but now knew about how to give and to love, about how to be loved and be given to.

It didn't matter that Autumn had had so many beers that she could scarcely stand, and it didn't matter that Autumn's walk had become a stumble, and it didn't even matter that Autumn would forget everything once she sobered up. All that mattered was that Evangelina still held deep inside the leaf-pile of her heart this one smoldering leaf, impossible to tamp down but lacking oxygen to ignite again, which maybe was for the best, was certainly easier that way, for Evangelina knew she could deny this one smoldering leaf until it died, starved of attention, of breath, of whatever was needed to make a smoldering leaf burst into flames and spread. She knew she could because she had done it before, but still, this time she hadn't.

Lying in bed with Russell's arms wrapped around her, his knees bent to fill the crook of her own, Evangelina wandered back to the feeling of Autumn's arms around her, to liking that they were not moving away from each other but just staying put, like they could have been glued together but weren't and knew the difference of being stuck together with adhesive and joined together with something else, though she didn't have a word for what that was, only knew that she could leave or Autumn could leave and that at any time this could happen and be okay, no questions asked, no explanation needed, which was maybe why it was that Evangelina had wanted to stay.

"I love you," Russell whispered into Evangelina's ear, and Evangelina felt herself wince at both his words and the heat of his breath, felt her body tense even as he scooted his body closer into hers as if he needed for them both to believe they were two perfectly matched spoons in a silverware drawer, though to Evangelina it felt like the only thing holding their mismatched souls together was some sort of glue spread wide and sticky along the front of his body to secure his body to her own.

Evangelina closed her eyes against Russell's closeness, relaxing only when she remembered the sound and feel of Autumn's "I love you" and remembered Autumn pulling back to look at her, remembered Autumn saying, "I don't know why I love you, but I do" before again giving herself to this embrace that had made Evangelina feel as though she and Autumn were two spoons, magnetically drawn together.

"Love you," Evangelina, pretending to be half asleep, half-murmured to Russell who had surprised her with "Tell me you love me," when she had not responded to his first "I love you," when her body—she knew—did not conform so easily as he would have wished to his. But she didn't know how these things could be anything other than what they were with Russell. Evangelina remembered reaching out and touching Autumn's cheek with her palm, remembered the sound of the words "I am so lonely" in Autumn's sad, sweet voice, remembered feeling then and feeling again even now with Russell's arms around her the depth of her own loneliness even as she said to Autumn, "You're so beautiful, Autumn," and then, "I'm here."

"I'm a good person. And I'm going to be okay, aren't I?" Autumn's breath against her neck. Evangelina closed her eyes, opened them.

Am I good enough for you to love me?

Have I done enough for you to be satisfied with me?

And suddenly Evangelina felt diminished, less-than, the closed part of a < equation on the other side of which was the greater-than crocodile mouth that could swallow the world and leave her all alone. She remembered Mrs. Selkirk's second grade less-than/greater-than math lesson, how her teacher had said, "Think of this sign as a crocodile mouth, and the crocodile as greater, as always hungry for more." She drew the < on the chalkboard, the white chalk scraping against the green board and a crocodile rose up through ocean mist, Captain Hook's pirate ship sailing through with Captain Hook leaning over the side and smiling because he believed himself in his red velvet finery on his Neverland ship to be greater-than. Evangelina had known then as she knew now that Hook wasn't a greater-than, wasn't even just enough, and she had watched the crocodile take shape, first its wide-open mouth followed by its sharp little triangle teeth along the upper and lower jaw.

As Mrs. Selkirk drew she said, "And all the numbers that are greater-than the number on the other side of this symbol can go here," and because Mrs. Selkirk wrote "9" on the other side, Evangelina kept writing 10, 11, 12, on her own paper, and then added "...". Evangelina knew that little et cetera of dots could go on forever and ever and ever and on up to infinity, which she knew was not a number in and of itself but that looked like an 8 sleeping on its side. Evangelina wished she could cover infinity with a blanket because she thought it must be so tired. So Evangelina drew on her paper the crocodile jaw just like Mrs. Selkirk's, then added to it one eye and a bumpy hide that extended all the way across its back on which could rest the 1, 2, 3, 4, 5, 6, and 7 as the tail slipped below the surface of the water, and before its open mouth the 9, 10, 11, and on and on and on.

Evangelina did not know whether she was in the crocodile's mouth, on its tail, or under water somewhere, but she knew she couldn't ever be a greater-than when she felt like such a less-than. Then Mrs. Selkirk drew 8=8 on the top of the crocodile's head and for Evangelina that was a picture of enough, enough being what Evangelina longed to be with its even and parallel lines, its symmetry, resting like a raft in an ocean. Evangelina longed to feel enough, which was not what she felt lying in bed with Russell's arms around her, but enough was what she had felt with Autumn last October, and what she had felt with Rose years before. With Autumn she had felt—she had known—she was enough. Not greater-than, not less-than, but enough. Enough to be held. Enough to be told "I love you." Enough to say to Autumn and also to herself, "You are beautiful. You will be okay. We will both be okay. I love you," and for that to be—in that moment and in this one too—enough.

Evangelina Looks at the Moon

One night when her mind and body were a clutter of thoughts and feelings, Evangelina knew herself to have been seen by the rising yellow moon so full and calm in its ocean of sky, and understanding herself to have been seen, Evangelina felt herself drawn back down to earth, to quiet, to a stillness that was also a motion, the planets and atoms and all of her always in motion, looking up to the sky and the moon rising full and yellow to pull her back into herself.

Evangelina Considers a Kiss

You can kiss me if you want to.

The cool clear voice of the woman sitting cross-legged on the beach, eyes once focused on the waves looked now into Evangelina, and in Evangelina's body, a now familiar spark, as Evangelina stood with her toes dug into the sand and her mind calm, the perpetual crash and roll of her thoughts paused as though for the first time and a notion . . . no . . . not at all a notion . . . not even a passing thought . . . nothing to mull over, consider, weigh, calculate, examine from every angle as she so often did, as she always did . . . no, not at all a notion but a spark, an impulse, a want, a desire unboxed and untethered.

You can kiss me if you want to.

This woman's voice bold, so bold, and Evangelina looked into eyes like yellow sunflowers surrounded by blue skies, eyes she wanted to feed on as though the pupils themselves were full of black seeds that could sustain her, but Evangelina knew eyes weren't food, knew her metaphor was odd, imperfect, and in her moment of knowing, Evangelina felt her familiar pull out of feeling and back into thought, feeling and thought always so at odds with each other in her, but her hunger—oh, her hunger!—and again her hunger in a wave crashed over her, so felt, so tremendous, and those sunflower eyes stripped Evangelina bare of her layers of thought and left her feeling naked, yes, but differently naked than the naked she'd known before, naked in a warm and full way of being seen.

You can kiss me if you want to.

That voice. Those eyes! And Evangelina longed now to be her own Cousteau, to plunge through those calm black pools, to dive deep and swim deeper still to explore this woman's Mindanao Trench, swim through her dark caverns where the blind fish lived, explore underwater worlds of ridged coral and rolling sands, the steadiness—always the steadiness—of this woman's eyes that held Evangelina captive here at Wrightsville Beach on this day in this moment at this one exact spot to find her here, here where her cousin Jo had brought her for an afternoon that felt like a forever.

You can kiss me if you want to.

And Evangelina, Evangelina met this woman's gaze with a gaze she knew to be hers, all her own, unflinching, bare, open, and Evangelina was not scared, not scared of this woman—never of this woman—for how could she ever be with this woman who looked at and saw her, saw *her*, whose seeing soothed Evangelina's seared mind like a cooling balm. Evangelina didn't know how that was, knew only that it was, that her endless bracing had eased and she smiled even as her eyes traced their own path from this woman's sunflower eyes down the length of her nose to her lips, lips so full and pink, and the woman biting just a little the corner of her lower lip with two slightly crooked teeth as if to stop her spreading smile, as if she were herself thinking of a kiss she wanted but would not be the one to claim.

You can kiss me if you want to.

Then within herself Evangelina felt herself pulling away from the journal she still held in her hands, the conch-shaped journal from Jo like the conch Evangelina had held as a child, like the conch that housed a nightlight in Jo's guest bedroom, like the conch from where she could always hear the ocean's roar, only this conch was made of cardstock and lined paper and Evangelina had all morning been trying to fill it with words that might echo back to her answers to all her many questions, words that would rescue her from her own mind, words that would put into order her whole world and life and history and body and keep her from changing.

You can kiss me if you want to.

Only now Evangelina did not feel herself to be a question to be answered, did not feel herself to be as she always had felt with Russell, some puzzle to solve or equation to be calculated out to the nth degree so that he might one day arrive at and contain the truth of her and so that she might one day know herself. But now she stood with her conch full of words and she had no new words to want to put into it, and no longer cared about the words already inside it, though knew she had had to write those words but now she no longer did. Now she only felt and did not need an answer, did not need to explain to this woman on the beach anything or even tell her name, her name which was so many names rolling inside of her in waves of *Evie, Eva, Eve, Evangelina,* and she all of them and less than them and more than them, and she just feeling how her skin felt from the inside.

You can kiss me if you want to.

This ocean, and Evangelina still stood with her toes dug into the sand.

This woman's face, this woman's body, the curve and lean of it as though she were a gentle lapping wave.

You can kiss me if you want to.

And Evangelina said, "I think I might like that."

Evangelina Watches the Sunrise

In the early morning quiet, Evangelina looked out over the waking town of Marietta, feeling everything.

She had risen with the sun, accepting this as both familiar and good for Evangelina had always felt most fully herself at sunrise. She was glad for her time again with Jo and glad for the woman on the beach who had said, "You can kiss me if you want to," and so Evangelina had, the woman's lips full and sweet, her body soft and beautiful, her smell like heat and salt and sweat. Evangelina smiled. Evangelina remembered that the woman had smiled too. And here before Evangelina now was the sun rising, rising because the world had not ended.

On this first day of August, this first day of the rest of her life, Evangelina stood before the Airbnb on Bellevue Street where she had landed the night before, knowing that what mattered was her belonging to herself. She was sure of this. Evangelina watched birds lift and dip and swoop and dive and rise again and felt that she too would ride the wind to the next stop on her journey.

Fully at rest and in motion, Evangelina listened to birdsong, cars, a passing train, a breeze through green leaves. Evangelina heard and smelled and saw the whole of it, inseparable. In the valley below, the Ohio River divided the states of Ohio and West Virginia, Evangelina thought, then let the thought go for she understood that some map maker may have drawn the mighty Ohio as the boundary between two states, but she knew the river was a flowing body, not a static line on a flat map. Evangelina knew that even the name Ohio that had been given to it could not contain all that it was.

Evangelina breathed in. Evangelina breathed out.

Evangelina felt it must be grace that had brought her to this prime space with this beautiful view on this exact morning to awaken in the world, the sun a vibrant orange that warmed and colored everything, even her, every day.

ACKNOWLEDGMENTS

*And it seemed to Evangelina that many people
helped love her into being.*

When I began writing *Evangelina Everyday*, I only meant to write one story, but after Evangelina had prayed for *Downton Abbey*, her voice stayed so I kept writing until her story became this book.

My creative communities provided starting points and testing grounds for these stories. Friends and fellow creatives from the Society for the Study of Midwestern Literature (SSML) and SwampFire Retreat for Writers and Artists saw *Evangelina Everyday* through from start to finish. The Syracuse Public Library Workshop became a welcome addition as I worked to refine the book for publication (special thanks to Sarah Wright for telling me about the Elkhart tooth brick!). I am honored to share the joys and challenges of writing with you all.

When I submitted my manuscript to Cornerstone Press, I thought I was sending publisher Ross Tangedal a finished product. I have never been more delighted to be wrong! The collaborative vision, insight, and patience of the editing and production teams has made *Evangelina Everyday* so much better. Special thanks to editorial director Kala Buttke, whose leadership helped shape this book into its final form while keeping me in the loop every step of the way. Thanks also to production director Amanda Leibham and her team for cover design. I am thankful for each team member's contribution and could not have wished for a better publishing experience.

My many friends and family loved my weird writer self through the writing of this book and they love me still. A few deserve special mention.

Tammy S. Gordon, to our enduring friendship formed on a long commute as adjunct instructors! I'm looking forward to the day our books are taught in the same college class. You inspire me!

Monica Heckel, you never minded my Evangelina intrusions and often egged me on. You left this world too soon, my square-peg-in-a-round-hole friend.

Saffron Goetschius, when my creative spark was sputtering, you were the catalyst who brought it flaming back. Thank you for music, mail, art, and friendship.

Andrea Baldwin, before we truly became friends, you asked to read my book and loved Evangelina whole—cluttered heart, overthinking mind, and all. I shall hope for other readers who love her half as much as you!

Elliot and Lucy, you are my joy and my light. I am so lucky to be your mom.

Bex, you are my heart, my home, my wife. Thank you for helping me find my best words even as you find your own. Moment by moment, I love you.

Mark and Cathy Owen, through Bex, you welcomed me into your family. With pride, you keep my writing on your bookshelf. I am so honored.

Mary Catherine Harper, for nearly two decades you have been ever present with support, insight, and love as a writer, a mentor, and a friend. You have made my life and this book more beautiful and more true than they ever could have been apart from you. Thank you.

Dawn Burns is the author of *A Green Glow on the Horizon* (Cornerstone Press 2026) and founder and co-organizer of the SwampFire community of writers and artists. An assistant professor at Michigan State University, Dawn is committed to writing and community building as acts of personal and social change.

www.ingramcontent.com/pod-product-compliance
Lightning Source LLC
Chambersburg PA
CBHW021732190726
48288CB00009B/3018